"To the one I love so very much:
thank you for your wisdom, patience, dedication and saying 'Yes.'
For now and forever."

—O.N.

First published in 2009 by Be Read
an imprint of Simply Read Books
www.simplyreadbooks.com

Text © 2009 Oliver Neubert
Cover © 2009 Atanas Atanassov

Library and Archives Canada Cataloguing in Publication

Neubert, Oliver, 1961-
Chantel's quest for the enchanted medallion / Oliver Neubert.

ISBN 978-1-897476-15-4

I. Title.

PS8623.E477C434 2009   jC813'.6   C2009-901955-8

We gratefully acknowledge for their financial support of our publishing program the
Canada Council for the Arts, the BC Arts Council, and the Government of Canada
through the Book Publishing Industry Development Program (BPIDP).

Printed in the United States of America   10 9 8 7 6 5 4 3 2 1

Oliver Neubert

CHANTEL'S QUEST
for the Enchanted Medallion

Be Read

WEST

The Four Lands

Table of Contents

CHAPTER ONE

Another Day

I am the past, I am the present and I am the future. Sometimes I walk with you. Sometimes I walk away from you. My name is Time, and all about me is written in this book. Those who write in here have experienced me and have the gift of telling the truth and seeing the future. They guide you, but they can never tell you all, because the whole truth might devastate you.

From The Book of Erebus

Chantel looked at the rune stone on the friendship bracelet Laluna had given her. Its glow was dull, a grayish blue, not silvery bright as before. When Chantel turned from the windows of her room that faced the land of the North, the rune stone turned completely black. Her shoulders slumped.

Chantel and Laluna had become very close during their journey north to the Mountain People. They'd battled Vampire Bats and traveled through snowstorms, journeyed through the Lake of Clouds, and discovered the City of Ice. They had met the friendly gargoyle Norfalk. They'd even escaped the Snow Walker unscathed—twice! But they hadn't evaded the Solenodon so soundly.

Chantel recalled all too well that dreadful evening when the Solenodon had attacked from the dark sky above the clearing and crushed Laluna's wing.

"Will Laluna ever be the same again? Will she be able to fly?" Chantel wondered, feeling helpless. "She will. She must. I have to stay hopeful. Despair is a sign of the Darkness. Mother Nature will help her. She must help her. If the wolves are right and Laluna is one of the four Winged Ones who can stop the Evil One, Laluna has to live. I would do anything to have Laluna back with me."

To take her mind off Laluna, Chantel turned to the table in the middle of her room. The Golden Sword, the relic of the North, lay on top of it. Chantel read the words that were engraved on the sharp golden blade: "For Us to Share."

She picked it up. The handle was still warm, just like the first time she'd touched it. The light and dark power pulsated in it. She remembered the applause of the elders when the Sword accepted her as the Princess of Freedom. She remembered using it against Aquila Bellum, the Snow Walker, and the transformation of Aquila's face into a woman's face— her mother's face. Most of all she remembered releasing the sword's light power, and how different that felt from releasing her Magic Staff's red lightning bolt.

"What am I supposed to do with the Sword now? I can't leave it here on my table while I'm away on my next journey," thought Chantel.

Touching the Sword brought back all the memories of her recent journey to the North and all the dangers she'd faced. As hard as it had been, there was one thing Chantel was sure about: she would never give up her quests. She would find the three other relics and free the four lands from the Evil One, even if it meant she had to give up her own life. But she continued to yearn to know, Who was the Evil One? Where was the Evil One hiding? And why was the Evil One trying to destroy all the lands?

"If only I'd asked her those questions when I had the chance," thought Chantel. "Hopefully she will speak to me again." But even as she thought this, she hoped she'd never again hear the Evil One's awful voice in her head.

Suddenly Chantel heard a voice—not the Evil One's but a different one, a strange humming voice—say, "It is time I show you."

Chantel spun around. "Who's there?"

She couldn't see anyone. Was an invisible enemy in her room? Dark thoughts filled Chantel's mind, and she was overcome with the urge to use the dark power in the Sword. Chantel closed her eyes. Her Golden Braid hung heavily from her head, a sign that the Darkness was close and influencing her thinking.

"Focus," she told herself. "Breathe. I am tired and worried about Laluna. I have been thinking about the Evil One. I am overreacting." After a few moments, in a much calmer voice, Chantel asked, "Who's there? Show yourself."

"Look out the window that faces north and you will see me, Princess," the voice said. "You will not need the Sword. I am not your enemy."

Chantel turned around.

A silver hummingbird hovered in front of her window. The bird was the same color as the silvery blue moon. All dark thoughts left Chantel's mind as she lowered the Sword.

"Mother Nature! I'm so glad to see you!"

"I'm sorry to disappoint you," the hummingbird answered politely, "but I am not Mother Nature. My color is silver, not gold, thus I am merely one of her messengers. Mother Nature is with Laluna. Laluna is not doing well."

Chantel's smile fell. "Is she dying?"

"I don't know," the hummingbird said, fluttering through the open window and landing on the chair beside the table, "but Mother Nature has to stay by her side. That's why I'm here instead of her. I came to show you something."

"Show me what?" Chantel whispered, still thinking about Laluna.

"Do you see the round rug under the table in the middle of your room? Move the table and the rug, and I will show you what you must do."

Chantel put the Sword down and followed the bird's instructions. Under the rug were four imprints in the floor that Chantel had never seen before. They were arranged in four quadrants surrounded by an octagon. A clear sheet that looked like it was made from ice or crystal covered the imprints and shimmered slightly. Chantel tapped it with her toe. It was hard.

"These imprints are the secret resting spots of the four relics. The Golden Sword faces north. The Silver Leaf faces east. The Enchanted Medallion faces south. And the Crystal Star faces west," the silver hummingbird explained. "You must place the Golden Sword into its imprint."

"But . . . shouldn't I remove the transparent sheet first?"

The hummingbird just pointed to the sheet with one of its wings. Chantel placed the Sword on top of the sheet, over its imprint. Immediately the Sword began to sink as if the sheet were liquid, until it came to rest in its imprint perfectly.

An indigo light shone around the golden relic. The Sword was so beautiful, its special features magnified by the transparent sheet, that Chantel wished to touch the Sword one last time. She reached down, expecting to be able to move through the sheet like the Sword had, but the sheet had hardened again and her hand bumped against the clear crystal.

"The sheet is an ancient protection made by Mother Nature. Each relic has its own protective color," the tiny bird explained. "Air is indigo, the color of the North. You will see the other colors later. I have to go now. Remember that all four relics are needed to free us from the Darkness, and the other three have to be placed in their imprints here in your tower."

The hummingbird moved her wings very quickly and lifted into the air.

"Please wait," Chantel said. "Tell me more about Laluna and Mother Nature."

Ignoring her request, the hummingbird said, "I sense that your dark side is tempting you. You have to be strong—very strong. You have touched the dark power, and it calls for you. I can hear it. Fight it, Princess. Fight it with all your might, or all will be lost."

With that, the hummingbird swiftly turned and flew through the open window towards the mountains. "Remember where you come from and all those who care for you," she whistled as she departed. "They believe in you."

"The mountains," Chantel said, following the flight of the hummingbird. "Nothing could make me forget that I am a mountain child."

Although she didn't know who her parents were, or even if they were still alive, on her last quest she had learned that her parents had been Mountain People, and she had felt a sense of belonging when traveling through the land of the North. Unfortunately, her next quest would take her in the opposite direction. As she pulled the rug back into its place, she glanced briefly at the round imprint of the southern relic.

"I wonder what its powers are," she thought.

After returning the table to its original position on the rug, she headed downstairs. Mouse, Owl and Fox would be waiting for her. Soon it would be time to leave on the next quest, the search for the Enchanted Medallion, and she had much to prepare.

CHAPTER TWO

The Wise One of the South

Even the strongest ones can lose their way.
It might not necessarily be due to the influence
of their dark side but due to the unforeseeable
forces of life. Often life redirects us without
giving us any choice. And then there are those
who lose their way in their attempt to escape
difficulty. Unfortunately, even if they find the
abyss of escape, they have left the important
things behind.

From The Book of Erebus

Deep in thought, Eno Esiw, the Wise One of the South, strode across the plateau of Storm Mountain, her hiding place since she was attacked eight moon crossings ago.

There was not a day that passed that she didn't think about what had happened.

She stopped walking when she reached the northern edge of Storm Mountain and looked towards the land of the North. She shivered. The desert was cold at night. The blood red moon was high and bright in the sky and the silvery blue moon was faint, just as they had been on that awful night eight moon crossings ago.

She prayed that the Last Descendant was safe. Mother Nature had told her that the Princess of Freedom would be journeying to the land of the South, but she hadn't told her when the Last Descendant would arrive. Before the attack, Eno wouldn't have had to rely on Mother Nature for such information. She used to be able to sense the future and her surroundings. She used to be in tune with the desert, its shifting sands and storms, and its creatures. She used to be in touch with all the desert tribes. But she hadn't left Storm Mountain since the Storm Riders had rescued her from the Sand Divers' ambush.

"I hope Mother Nature warned the Last Descendant about the Sand Divers. But what if she didn't?" Eno wondered. Looking down at her friend, a little sand cat, Eno asked, "Tac, will you please go north to the border? The Last Descendant is coming soon. You have to greet her and bring her safely to me."

Eno had found Tac in the desert and had saved the little animal's life. Since that day, Tac hadn't left Eno's side.

"I will go," Tac answered, "but how will I know it is the Last Descendant?"

"Look for the Golden Braid. That is the sign of the Last

Descendent. Be careful, Tac. I am counting on you."

The orange cat jumped into Eno's outstretched arms and gave her a quick lick before jumping down again. "I will find the one you describe and escort this Last Descendant here safely. I promise."

CHAPTER THREE

Breakfast

In the kitchen, Fox and Mouse were already at the old wooden table enjoying their breakfasts. Fox was perched on a bowl of grapes and busy eating. Seated on his haunches, Mouse was nibbling on a slice of toast that was almost as big as he was.

Owl, standing beside the fireplace near the window that faced the courtyard, was busy fixing Chantel's favorite breakfast: scrambled eggs. Fin, the Wise One of the North, was the only one in the kitchen sitting still, doing nothing. He was hunched in an old chair in the corner beside the window, his face hidden between his knees, which he had brought up close to his chest. It looked like he was sleeping, but Chantel's senses told her that he was awake and listening.

Mouse gulped down a big chunk of bread. "Good morning, Chantel," he said.

Fox simply nodded since his mouth was full.

"The eggs are almost ready," Owl said, "and there's tea on the table."

Chantel sat near Mouse and Fox and poured tea into her favorite mug. She looked at Mouse and motioned her head towards Fin as if to ask, "What's wrong with him?" Mouse shrugged his shoulders and pointed to the door that led into the courtyard.

"We're just going outside for some fresh air," Chantel said, setting down her tea. Owl knew what was going on but didn't say a word. Mouse got up, jumped off the table and followed Chantel outside.

"Fin isn't happy that his mind's been closed," Mouse said to Chantel when they reached the big tree in the center of the castle's small garden. "He hasn't eaten any breakfast. He hasn't even sipped tea or smoked his pipe like he used to in his cave in the mountains."

The leaves on the maple trees that lined the walkway had already changed from green to a light red, announcing the end of summer and the beginning of fall. The grass was still green, but some areas, especially those closest to the castle's protective wall, had started to turn brown, a sign that the Darkness was getting closer.

"But I had to close his mind! He attacked me last night!" exclaimed Chantel.

"I know," said Mouse. They both remembered how Fin's dark side had taken over and how he had grown so jealous of Chantel's abilities that he had tried to kill her.

"You had no other choice," Mouse reassured her. "If his mind is open and he allows jealousy to take hold again, he could use his telepathic abilities to contact the Evil One and give away the location of the castle. We can't risk that."

"What should we do with him?"

"Leave him here with Owl. Owl will look after him."

"Are you sure?"

Mouse looked surprised. The whiskers below his pointy nose twitched slightly.

"What do you mean?" he asked, stepping closer to Chantel, knowing that she was about to say something important and not wanting to miss a word.

"There is something about Owl that's troubling me," Chantel continued quietly, bending down to Mouse. "I sense that he's hiding a secret."

"Well, he did want to tell you something. Something about Etam Luos and the South."

Etam Luos. The name trilled in Chantel's mind. Etam, the man who lived in the desert and who'd visited her in a vision. Her Soul Mate! Her worries of Fin and Owl faded as Mouse added, "Come on. Let's go back inside. I'll bet your eggs are ready."

"Perfect timing," Owl said, setting down two plates of steaming eggs on the table, one for Chantel and one for himself.

Fin was no longer sitting in the old chair. He had moved to the bench at the table, but he was still in the same crouched position. Chantel sat down. Fin slowly lifted his head and looked at her. In his eyes Chantel saw a deep, endless helplessness. She felt sorry for Fin but knew that she had to be careful. She picked up her fork.

"Release me," Fin whispered. His voice was like a hiss.

Chantel's fingers trembled and she dropped her fork, but she said calmly, "Speak up if you want to say something. Whatever you have to say, say it so all of us can hear you."

"Release me," Fin said louder, his teeth clenched so tightly that his jawbones stuck out. "I know what you have done to me. I can't sense danger anymore. I can't hear thoughts anymore. I can't feel emotions anymore. I can't feel me anymore. You are killing me slowly. Release me from your spell and open the doors to my mind again."

"I'm sorry, Fin, but I won't," said Chantel. "I can't. You're a danger to us all. I wish there were some other way. I'm still your friend and I will try to help you, but first you have to help yourself. Be strong and do not listen to your dark side. I can't open the doors to your mind yet, not until you have proven that you are no longer jealous of those who have knowledge you do not. Remember, knowledge is 'For Us to Share.' Do you remember those words engraved in the blade of the Golden Sword? Do you remember what they mean?"

"'For Us to Share,'" Fin repeated quietly to himself, looking at the ground. Then he jerked his head up. "Where is the Golden Sword?" he demanded, staring at Chantel. "I have to see it again." All of a sudden his voice changed again and he began to plead, "Please show it to me so that I can believe." A faint, mad smile crossed his face.

"I can't show it to you, Fin," Chantel replied. "It's no longer in my possession."

Mouse and Owl looked at each other in surprise.

"You're lying!" Fin's voice turned to a shout. "You're a deceitful little girl. It's you we should be fearful of. The Evil One has got hold of you. That's why you released the red lightning bolt of the Darkness."

"I did not!" replied Chantel. "I released it to save Laluna from the Solenodon! There was no other way."

Fin's face turned red and he jumped up in his seat, ready to hurdle over the table to attack Chantel, but someone grabbed Fin's shoulder and forced him back into his seat. Tiny Mouse had transformed instantaneously into the Mighty Warrior. His muscular chest was covered in black armor and fastened to a leather belt around his waist was a long, sharp sword. His paws were huge and bared sharp claws.

"'For Us to Share,'" Chantel repeated calmly. "Remember, Fin." She turned to Owl. "What should we do?"

"The Darkness is strong in him. Although the doors to his mind are closed, we can't risk him running away and finding Aquila Bellum. We must isolate him. Do not worry. I know a place where he can stay here in the castle, where he will be safe."

Owl got up and walked over to Fin, who was back in his crouched position, hiding his face behind his knees. "Come with me, Fin," Owl said. When Fin didn't move, Owl hooted. The noise sent shivers up Chantel's spine. She had never heard this hoot before.

Fin finally got up. He followed Owl out of the kitchen, slumped over so much that his long, gray beard trailed on the floor.

Chantel, Mouse, and Fox finished their breakfasts quietly, all thinking about the old Fin who was intelligent and colorful, a true Wise One. He had let them stay in his cozy cave in the mountains and taught and guided them on their first quest.

"If only I could help him now," thought Chantel. "I am supposed to be the Princess of Freedom, and look at what I am doing: I am imprisoning someone I love."

Chantel's thoughts were interrupted when Owl returned alone.

"Where did you put him?" Mouse asked.

"He's safe now," Owl answered. "That's all you need to know. Let me worry about Fin. You have to get ready for your journey to the South."

As Owl began to eat his cold eggs, Chantel was once again troubled by something. Her Golden Braid hung with more weight than usual and hurt her temples. If only she knew what her senses were warning her about.

Before she could ask Owl any questions, he spoke. "I have been thinking about Etam Luos, and although I don't know much, it is important that I tell you all I know before you leave. In fact, no one knows much about Etam. But this is what I do know: Like Aurora, the leader of the Northern Mountain People, Etam is also a leader. He is the leader of the Southern tribes. But he is a very different sort of leader than Aurora. Then again, the desert is a very different sort of place."

Owl paused to take a sip of tea and a mouthful of egg.

"The desert is unfriendly," he continued after a while, "scorching during the day and freezing during the night. The desert folk travel in tribes in search of water and food, both of which are scarce. They are constantly occupied with survival. This gives them keen senses and sharp minds. All the tribes have a chief, but all the chiefs look up to Etam Luos, who moves around as much as they do. Unlike them, however, he moves alone from one tribe to the next, making sure all the tribes are fine. That is why you may have difficulty finding him.

"The desert's relic, the Enchanted Medallion, represents simplicity, the lifestyle of the Desert People. Simplicity means that one is happy with what one has. The dark power within the Medallion, on the other hand, will change that value system and those beliefs. Simplicity will change to greed, gluttony and selfishness. In the hands of the Darkness, the Medallion can create wealth and control others.

"The Desert People don't want excessive belongings because such things would only hinder them on their travels. But it doesn't mean that the idea of a luxurious life can't influence them.

"Just like Aquila Bellum, the Warlord of the North, who pursued you to get his hands on the Golden Sword, there is a Warlord of the South who desires the Enchanted Medallion. He and his evil ones are sure to hunt for you."

"What about Aquila?" asked Chantel. "Where do you think he's gone? Doesn't he also want the Enchanted Medallion?"

"I'm not sure," said Owl. "But from what you have told me about his defeat, Aquila is certain to want revenge. So you must be careful, my dear, for you may well have two warlords pursuing you on your quest to the South."

CHAPTER FOUR

Aquila Bellum

Good and evil have been enemies since the beginning of time. And they will continue to be so until the end of time, but sometimes, there is light in the darkness and what was once forgotten will resurface again. This will start a battle within oneself that can only be won when one is willing to discover what one has forced oneself to forget.

From The Book of Erebus

Aquila Bellum was in his cave high up in the mountains. He had received word from his spies, the screeching crows, and he knew now where Chantel had been seen last. He had also been informed that Chantel had met the wolves from the Northwest. Aquila did not fear the wolves. He didn't fear anything.

On his map of the four lands, he marked Chantel's trail. The first mark on the map was where he had met Chantel in the mountains. The next one was where he had discovered Fin's cave behind the waterfall. The third one was where Chantel had released the red lightning bolt of the Darkness that killed his friend, the monstrous Solenodon. He still could not comprehend how Chantel had been able to wield the dark power of the Golden Sword and live. When he had released the lightning bolt, his hands had been badly burned.

"No human is strong enough to handle so much power," he thought. "All those who tried before died a miserable, painful death, except me."

The last mark on his map was where Chantel had been seen last. The screeching crows told him that she'd disappeared. He was not worried. Chantel, the Princess of Freedom, would resurface. She still had to retrieve three more relics, and when she tried, he would be ready.

Aquila folded his map and put it back on a shelf and then turned to his fireplace, where a fire crackled. The previous night's snow covered the mountains with a thin white blanket, and the temperature had dropped accordingly. In front of the fireplace, two of Aquila's big wolverines lay on the ground, licking wounds they'd received during the fight with the Mighty Warrior.

Aquila sat in his big chair and closed his eyes, preparing to contact his three counterparts in the other lands with his mind. He had to make sure that they knew about Chantel and her powers and weapons. But he found it difficult to concentrate. His thoughts kept drifting to the memories of his encounter with the Princess of Freedom.

Like his wolverines, he'd been injured in the fight, too. His right side still hurt from the impact of the white lightning bolt Chantel had released. He lifted his shirt. A white scar had formed on his chest where the bolt had struck him. It was the shape of a child's hand. Aquila had many scars from many fights but none as strange as this one.

He knew that it was Chantel's hand that had touched him. When he examined the scar closely, he could see it pulsating, almost as if the scar itself were alive. Strangest of all, the scar remained constantly warm to the touch, and he could feel the warmth spreading throughout his body, a warmth he hadn't felt for the longest time.

He remembered feeling this warmth when he was a fifteen-year-old boy and his father had praised him for surviving a trip designed to test the strength of twenty-year-old men. He remembered feeling this warmth when his mother had gushed over his gift of the rare edelweiss flowers, her favorite flower because of its sweet, earthy scent. And he remembered feeling this warmth when he'd rescued his little sister from the torrents of a mighty glacial river.

Aquila yanked his shirt down.

"What's happening to me?" he cried. "What did that awful girl do to me? I must stop it!" His words echoed in the cave. His wolverines looked up for a second and then returned to licking their wounds.

But his words did not stop his scar from pulsating. He stood up and strode to the cave entrance.

Outside, the wind howled and large snowflakes flew through the air. As he'd hoped, the cold air began to clear his mind. He breathed in and out slowly, and he returned to being the Snow Walker again, the man without mercy, the Warlord of the North, the ally of the Evil One.

Then he heard a voice in his head. "Chantel will go south," the voice rasped. Aquila knew that voice well. It was the Evil One.

"How do you know this?" asked Aquila.

"Let's just say a little bird told me," the Evil One replied. "Get ready to follow her. Contact the Warlord of the South and warn him. He is a weak warlord. He still has feelings for the Wise One of the South and Etam Luos. His alliance to the Darkness is faltering. I trust this is not happening to you, Aquila. You have always been my most loyal warlord . . ." The Evil One's voice began to fade away.

"I will always stay true to you!" said Aquila, waiting and listening for a response, but the Evil One failed to reply.

⟶𝄞⟵

The Evil One was standing alone on her little island, surrounded by red mist. She knew that Aquila had been touched by the light power and she felt that he was changing. Their alliance was weakening. If Aquila would not retrieve the four relics, she would have to do it herself. She yanked her right foot forward, and the magic glass chain that was tightly secured around her ankle clattered across the rocky ground.

"One last chain," the Evil One thought. "Once that one is broken, I will be free again."

⟶𝄞⟵

Aquila went into his cave, thinking about his counterpart in the desert. Enim Ymene was the leader of the Sand Divers, creatures that were able to live deep in the sand, where no one could see or detect them. To eliminate their enemies, the Sand Divers would drag them under the sand and hold them there until they suffocated. It was a brutal death. Even Aquila Bellum shuddered when he thought about it.

As deadly as the Sand Divers were, Aquila knew he had to warn them of Chantel's strength, especially if Enim was weak. He closed his eyes and began to focus. This time, perhaps because of the cold or the Evil One's words, Aquila was able to contact him, without the intrusion of any annoying memories.

CHAPTER FIVE

Another Farewell

Leaving home is always hard, but if home
is shrouded in a mist of distrust and fear,
the sound of the closing door behind you will
set you free. No longer will you have to look
over your shoulder in a place that should be
providing you with sanctuary.

From The Book of Erebus

In the castle's kitchen, Owl continued to tell Chantel about her quest to the South. Mouse and Fox listened, too.

"It will be difficult for you to find Etam Luos, even though he is your Soul Mate," said Owl. "The Evil One is keeping Soul Mates apart. You must find Etam because his help is crucial to finding the Enchanted Medallion."

"I will find him," Chantel said confidently. "But what about the Wise One of the South?"

"She came to this castle and retrieved the Enchanted Medallion eight moon crossings ago, when all the Wise Ones came here to retrieve their relics. Since then no one has heard from her. There are rumors that on her way back to the desert, the Warlord of the South captured and tortured her. He may have even killed her. But the Warlord, I'm sure, didn't get the Medallion; otherwise he would control the desert by now. I wish I could tell you more or where to begin your search. All I know for sure is that this quest will be more difficult and longer than the previous one."

"Then we should set out immediately," said Chantel. "Every moment we delay we grow closer to the next moon crossing and the final moment when we must release the light power. I will get my things and meet you at the door."

Back in her room, Chantel gazed at the golden desert through her window facing south. Even though it was far off in the distance, the sun's reflection on the golden sand was so bright that Chantel had to shield her eyes with her hands.

"I wonder what Etam's like and how we are connected," she thought, and with that thought came the worry, "Will we even like each other?"

Chantel closed her eyes. Etam Luos had come to her in a vision just before she'd released the red lightning bolt that killed the Solenodon. Etam had contacted her to guide her in her time of greatest need and helped her release the red lightning bolt in such a way that its power couldn't tear her apart.

"If he was able to contact me then, maybe I can contact him now," thought Chantel, recalling Etam's face.

"Etam?" she whispered.

There was no reply. The wind outside her tower whistled slightly.

"Etam," she whispered again, "can you hear me?" She listened intently, hoping for a word, a sign—anything.

Then all of a sudden a faint voice echoed in her mind. "Chantel?"

Her heart beat quickly. "Etam!"

"I can hear you, Chantel." Etam Luos's voice was soft and gentle. "How did you find me?"

"I thought about the vision and about your face. How did you find me?"

"I heard your voice in my mind."

"But how did you find me the first time, when I was battling the Solenodon?"

"I don't know how," replied Etam. "I was just about to go to sleep, when I had a terrible feeling that someone I loved needed my help. When I closed my eyes, I saw you facing the Solenodon and holding your Staff. Your grave danger must have overcome the Evil One's power to keep us apart. I could feel you so vividly; it was as if I were standing next to you. I feel that same way right now."

"Me, too," said Chantel.

"When we meet, we will find out what makes us Soul Mates," added Etam.

"Where?" Chantel thought. "Where can I find you?"

There was no answer.

"Etam?"

"I sense the Evil One is close. She may be listening to our conversation. We must be very careful. Good-bye for now, Chantel." His voice faded away.

Chantel stood at her window for a few moments, delighting in the fact that she had just contacted her Soul Mate but at the same time worrying about the constant threat of the Evil One. Chantel took a breath and freed herself from her worries and got ready to leave her castle.

She changed into layers of light cotton clothing, pulled on her leather boots, and fastened to her belt her small silver sword, her Magic Staff, and her purple pouch filled with an assortment of herbs. She said a quick farewell and ran down the stairs.

At the castle doors she met Mouse, Fox and Owl. Mouse and Fox were ready to leave, too.

"What took you so long?" Mouse asked. "Couldn't say good-bye to the gorgeous view?"

Chantel smiled back at her loyal friend but didn't give any explanation. She looked at Owl, knowing that he would stay behind again, especially now that Fin was in the castle. Owl handed Chantel a heavy backpack filled with fruit, sausage, bread and cheese. He also gave her a water container made of leather hide.

"It was a present from Mother Nature many moon crossings ago. It continuously fills with fresh water. As long as you carry it, you will never go thirsty. And here," Owl said, handing her a bright yellow cloak. "This will reflect the heat of the day and keep you warm during the cold nights in the desert."

"Thank you, Owl." Chantel removed her old cloak and tied on the new one and gave Owl a big hug.

Mouse jumped into Chantel's cloak pocket and Fox flew up and landed on Chantel's shoulder. Chantel took out her

Magic Staff and remembered the ancient writings: "Water: Swimming in invisibility? You will rise again."

As she concentrated on the color blue, the power filled her body, making her feel fluid and free. Soon she, Mouse and Fox vanished. They were invisible.

"Be careful," said Owl.

"We will," replied Chantel.

Owl watched as first the big wooden castle doors and then the iron gates on the south side of the castle wall opened and closed. Chantel, Mouse and Fox were gone.

Owl turned around and walked back into the empty kitchen. His wings, which he had been squeezing tightly to his sides, relaxed. He was relieved that he was alone again. Since learning of Laluna, he'd been constantly on edge.

The news that some of the Winged Ones had survived was wonderful but worrisome. Did Laluna or any of the other surviving Winged Ones remember the Wise One of the West? Did any of them wonder why the Wise One hadn't been there to protect them from the red lightning bolt?

Owl was grateful and hoped that none of the remaining Winged Ones would recognize him. "Surely they won't," he thought. "Not even Fin recognized me."

As he cleaned up the kitchen table and washed the dishes, he watched the birds in the old maple trees through the open window. They picked away at the bark, looking for insects and grubs. How carefree they looked!

"If only I could be a simple bird, without any concerns, commitments or confusion."

But Owl had never been a simple bird. The moment he cracked out of his eggshell, the spirits selected him to be the Wise One of the West. How special he'd felt! When he was just a tiny owlet, ninety moon crossings ago, he swore an oath to the Spirit of the West that he would always be true to his people, the Winged Ones, and always serve the Spirit of the West as a helper and link between the spirit world and the human world.

At that time he never dreamt that the Spirit of the West would turn into the Evil One. And he had never thought Mother Nature would make him swear another oath to protect the Princess of Freedom.

Mother Nature hadn't known then, and still didn't know today, of his secret bond to the Spirit of the West. If Mother Nature knew, she certainly wouldn't have let him be Chantel's guardian. And that was a terrible thought, because Owl loved Chantel more than anyone in the world. He would stay true to his oath to Mother Nature, but what about his oath to the Spirit of the West?

"The Evil One hasn't asked me to harm Chantel yet. But what happens if she does? What will I do then?"

CHAPTER SIX

Enim Ymene

No one can escape his or her past—not the most Evil One nor the Last Descendant. Before the end and before the whole truth is known, one evil one will seek his good side and one good one will be tempted by her dark side. When you are as close as brother and sister, only one side can win in the end.

From The Book of Erebus

"**Enim!** This is Aquila, the Warlord of the North!"

Enim Ymene heard Aquila Bellum's voice in his head. He scowled, annoyed to be interrupted during his midday rest. He was lying in a small tent surrounded by his army of Sand Divers. The air in the tent was stale and smelled like old sweaty socks. He sat up and took a sip from a glass filled with water. It was warm. He hadn't slept well the previous night, haunted by dreams of what he had done to the Wise One of the South. He was filled with sorrow and sadness, and he missed the friendship and trust he used to have with Eno Esiw.

"What do you want, Aquila?" Etam thought, irritated.

"I have important news for you," Aquila thought back. "Chantel, the Princess of Freedom, is on her way to the desert. You must get ready."

"You don't have to warn me," he thought. "I'm not weak like you. You can't even capture one little girl."

"She is no mere little girl," Aquila Bellum responded angrily. "She has the will and power to release the red lightning bolt of the Darkness, and she is in possession of the Magic Staff."

"Yes, yes. I know all that. The Evil One speaks to me as well. Don't worry your little mind, Aquila. I will make our master proud. If you wish, I will even give you her Golden Braid as a gift."

Aquila blocked Enim Ymene out of his thoughts.

"So this arrogant desert crawler thinks he's so powerful? Ha! Just wait until he meets the Princess. Just wait until she attacks him! He'll be begging for mercy." Aquila laughed. He almost felt proud of Chantel. "In fact, I'd like to see him like that! And after he's been destroyed, I can capture her for the Evil One myself. Yes, that is what I will do."

He stood up. His face was red and he was aching to do something. He was longing to go south. His instincts pushed him to go on a hunt—a hunt for the Last Descendant.

"Maybe with her death this warmth and these stupid memories will go away."

He filled his pack with food—mostly frozen meat—and grabbed his gray cloak, sword and bow and arrows.

"Come," he said abruptly, looking at his wolverines, but only one got up. The other one was trying to stand but his injured leg kept giving way. Aquila kneeled down to him and touched his head.

"Stay, my friend, and rest some more. Anyway, you have to stay behind and guard the cave."

The wounded wolverine answered with a thankful growl.

Outside the cave, the storm had calmed. On a snow-dusted tree branch, a red-tailed mountain bird sang a love song. The song sounded very similar to the welcoming song of the Mountain People. Aquila caught himself humming it before he realized what he was doing. He bit his tongue and scowled.

"Away!" he cried, pointing an arrow at the bird.

The bird jumped from the branch and flew into the mountains. Aquila turned in the opposite direction—south, towards the desert.

CHAPTER SEVEN

The Journey South

Chantel hurried down the hill and away from the castle. She did not want to use the power of the Staff for too long because it drained so much of her inner strength, but she had to make sure that they stayed invisible until they were far enough away that nobody could connect them to the location of the castle.

Finally after a few minutes of intense marching, she reached a tall green bush with yellow leaves and red berries. Behind it she released her spell, and she and her friends became visible again.

As the power left her, her knees trembled. She leaned against a tree to steady herself. Fox leapt into the air, stretching his wings. Mouse jumped out of her cloak pocket.

"Are you okay?" Mouse asked.

Chantel nodded. "I will be in a moment," she said, resting for a bit as she gazed at the castle. But all she could see was a misty hill.

"If we're lucky, we'll reach the outskirts of the desert in two and a half days," Mouse said. "I know an excellent tree to sleep in tonight, but it's quite far away. Are you strong enough to continue?"

"Yes," replied Chantel.

Chantel followed Mouse with a smile, happy to be journeying in nature again, freed from the feeling of suspicion and mistrust she felt in her own castle.

"It is so nice to be free of the castle. I felt so uncomfortable in there, as if I was surrounded by darkness," she thought. "It was probably all because of Fin."

She breathed in deeply. The air was fresh; the leaves on the trees were beginning to turn yellow and orange, the colors of sand.

The path they took reminded her of her first journey. It first led farther downhill and then turned into the forest that surrounded the hill where her castle stood. After walking for a few hours through the forest, they reached a clearing. When Chantel stepped out of the dense woodland and into the open grassland, she froze, instantly reminded of the clearing where the monstrous Solenodon had attacked Laluna. A vision of Laluna lying lifeless and bloodied in the grass filled her mind.

She felt a paw on her shoulder. She jumped and screamed.

"It's just me, Chantel!" said the Mighty Warrior. Mouse had changed into the giant armored mouse so quickly and silently that she hadn't even noticed. "You're safe. Nothing will happen here." Gently, he guided her through the clearing. "Three more hours and we will reach the special tree I told you about," he added.

"Thank you, Mouse," Chantel said. She looked at her friendship bracelet and touched the cool stone mounted on it. "Laluna, I wish you were here."

Mouse was right. The special tree was beautiful. It was a giant gnarled oak with branches so high up that it looked like its top was touching the sky. Its leaves glimmered green with a slight touch of yellow and red in the falling sun.

"This will be the last big tree for a long time," Mouse said. "From tomorrow on, shade will be scarce."

As the sun settled, the three travelers perched high in the tree, enjoying the meal that Owl had packed for them. After admiring a breathtaking, colorful sunset, each of them found a separate branch to sleep on.

Chantel pointed her friendship bracelet towards the mountains. The rune stone flickered faintly. Then she turned to the South. In the distance, hills and mountains of sand swelled against the dark horizon. The stars above sparkled, and the two moons walked their nightly path across the endless universe.

CHAPTER EIGHT

Laluna

Laluna was barely breathing, and her sweaty skin had started to turn blue. Mother Nature crouched beside her, holding her hand. It was small and soft compared to Mother Nature's, which was rough like bark and sinewy like roots.

Laluna's breath rasped in her throat.

Mother Nature closed her eyes. "This will hurt, my little Laluna, but it will make you breathe again," she whispered.

She began to hum quietly. The candles in the cave darkened and the air became cold. Her humming became louder, and then she started to sing. She called upon the healing strength of nature and of forgiveness over time. The violet candle beside Laluna started to flicker violently and seemed certain to blow out, but it didn't.

Slowly a soft white veil, like the shimmering web of a silkworm, began to wrap around Laluna's body until she looked like a giant cocoon. The air in the cave became busy with movement as thousands of fireflies flew down from the ceiling and settled on the soft fabric covering Laluna. Then all their little tails lit up at once, sending a shock through Laluna's body.

Her body moved violently up and down a few times, and the veil that covered her started to rip apart. Her eyes and mouth burst open and she inhaled deeply.

Laluna sat up for a second and then fell back onto her mossy bed. Gradually her breathing became calm and regular again. Her skin color slowly turned back to a soft light brown. Mother Nature, who was still sitting beside her and holding her hand, could feel the blood rushing though Laluna's veins.

Letting go of Laluna's hand, Mother Nature stood up and covered her with a light blue silk blanket.

"What happened?" Laluna whispered weakly.

"You were on your way to the afterworld, but you returned. Rest, my child. I will be back in a second."

The rune stone on Laluna's friendship bracelet started to glow. The glow gave her heart strength. She knew what it meant; Chantel was thinking about her.

Mother Nature returned with a cup of tea, which she held to Laluna's lips. Laluna took a few small sips and swallowed carefully.

"How do you feel?" Mother Nature asked.

"I can't feel my right wing."

"The tea will help. Your fever has broken, and soon you will be able to walk."

"Will I ever fly again?" Laluna asked, tears filling her eyes.

"I'm not sure," said Mother Nature gently. "Your wing is still badly damaged. Time will tell how well it heals. I will leave this tea here for you to finish. There are other creatures I must tend to, but I will be back soon."

Laluna drank the tea and lay back on her bed.

The violet candle beside her burned fiercely. Laluna watched the reflection of the flame dancing in the many crystals that covered the cave's ceiling. Hundreds of little lights flickered from the crystals—one light for each injured creature Mother Nature was looking after.

Laluna's rune stone had stopped glowing.

Laluna missed Chantel so much. Chantel was like a sister to her. She was Laluna's only family now, since the red lightning bolt had destroyed her village.

"I am the last of the Winged Ones," Laluna whispered to herself, "the last of the Winged Ones, with only one good wing."

CHAPTER NINE

A New Sense

"Wake up, sleepyheads!" Mouse clamored. "The sun is already out of its bed. It's going to be a wonderful day!"

"I'm up, Mouse." Chantel yawned. "Do you have to yell so loudly? You're going to wake up everybody in the four lands."

Chantel climbed down the tree and ate a quick breakfast of bread left over from last night's dinner. She was eager to continue their journey.

By the time the sun had reached its highest point in the sky, they were traveling across an area Mouse called the steppe. It was the flat land that formed the transition between the land of the North and the land of the South, where the abundant green of the North turned into small brown bushes and sand.

"No more moss and grass to lie on and no more trees to climb," Chantel thought. She already missed the trees. She closed her eyes and wiped the sweat off her forehead, remembering the cool snow of the mountains.

With the breeze that blew in from the North came a horrible scream. The air suddenly filled with tension, and Mouse changed into the Mighty Warrior and stood close to Chantel. Fox jumped onto her shoulder.

"What was that?" Chantel asked in a whisper. Looking around, she could only see shrubs, brown sand and the blue sky.

"It's the sound of the winged hunters," Mouse replied, "mountain creatures that listen only to the Evil One. They are far away from their home."

"Solenodons?" Chantel asked, trembling.

"No," Fox said. "Solenodons would never fly this far away from the mountains. And their scream has a higher pitch to it, a horrible scream that will make your skin go numb."

Still, Chantel sensed the presence of something extremely evil. She gripped her Magic Staff tightly. She also felt a sensation she had never experienced before. The crystal of her Magic Staff pulsated in orange, one of the Evil One's colors, but Chantel didn't see it. Her head ached and her sight blurred. The Mighty Warrior pulled his sword out of its sheath. The metallic sound screeched in her ears. All her senses intensified. Every sound hurt. The slight breeze that crossed the steppe felt like hundreds of sharp little needles penetrating her skin.

Chantel began to twitch. She tried to concentrate and understand what was happening to her. She shook her head and then, as if through a lifting fog, she saw the land far below her. She felt the wind in her face and heard the flapping sound of wings. The Mighty Warrior called out to her, but she didn't hear him. She was flying high in the blue sky. Below her she saw a tall, muscular creature holding a long sword. Beside him stood a girl with a Fox Bat on her shoulder.

"That's me!" Chantel cried. "Mouse, look up! I am flying above you!"

The Mighty Warrior gazed up in horror. "Screeching crows!" he cried, lifting his sword high and swinging it above his head.

Chantel looked around. There were wings, claws, beaks, a flurry of black feathers and high-pitched cries. She was in the midst of the vicious hunters of the North. Suddenly she realized that she was actually looking at herself and her friends below through the eyes of an enemy. Chantel's hand instinctively clutched the cold wooden Staff. The Staff began to pulsate. The power in it grew stronger and stronger, and suddenly she was back on the ground, seeing the world through her own eyes again.

The crows were all around her. Some were already lying dead on the ground, slain by the Mighty Warrior's sword. Fox had attached himself to one attacker and was cutting through its black feathers with his sharp claws. Several crows landed on the Mighty Warrior's shoulder and pecked viciously at his neck.

The Mighty Warrior screamed in pain and clawed them off. Five more landed on him. Blood began to flow down his fur from several puncture wounds. Chantel swung her sword and stabbed some of the screeching creatures, killing them instantly, but there were thousands more and the blue sky above turned dark, packed with the evil creatures. The day became night.

Chantel's mind worked quickly. She gripped her Staff

even tighter, and the orange light burst forth. Again she saw the world from the eyes of one of their winged enemies. She knew what she had to do. The enemy's vision was much more sensitive than her own, and she knew what they feared most: fire. Chantel thought of the color yellow and about the many sunflowers that grew around her castle. Her viewpoint returned to her own body. She remembered the yellow cape Owl had given her to generate warmth. The power of yellow—of fire—grew strong, and warmth began to radiate from her. With a sudden burst, flames emerged from the end of her Staff and shot into the sky.

The crows screeched so loudly that Chantel felt as though her ears would explode.

And then they were gone.

The air was full of smoke and the smell of burnt feathers, and the sun shone brightly again in the blue sky.

Chantel lay on the ground with the Mighty Warrior kneeling beside her and Fox sitting on her chest.

"Chantel, wake up!" the Mighty Warrior said as he grabbed the water bottle attached to her belt, opened it, and splashed some cold water on her face.

Chantel slowly opened her eyes. "What happened?" she murmured, her head still pounding with pain.

"You'd better tell us, Chantel," the Mighty Warrior replied. "You shot out fire, and the crows that were still alive flew off. Many are dead."

"I saw everything through the eyes of a crow," Chantel said as she sat up, "and I sensed what they were feeling: their anger, fears and desires. That's how I knew that fire would work. They're scared to death of it. They aren't bad—not really. Something or someone was controlling them."

"The Darkness!" the Mighty Warrior said.

"Yes, the Darkness. It controls people and sees inside them. That's what the Evil One does. I'm am not an Evil One, am I?" Chantel looked up at the Mighty Warrior and Fox.

Fox flew back onto her shoulder and pressed his head against her cheek.

"Fox doesn't think so." The Mighty Warrior smiled and helped Chantel up. "And neither do I."

"It did help us," Chantel whispered, "seeing the world through our enemies' eyes."

The Mighty Warrior didn't hear her. All his attention was focused on his still-bleeding wounded neck, which he held with one of his paws.

"Let me have a look at that," Chantel said.

"It is not that bad. You know that I heal quickly when I am the Mighty Warrior." He stepped away from Chantel, preventing her from taking a closer look. "Come," he said, looking back at Chantel. "We still have a half day of light left. Let's get going."

CHAPTER TEN

The Desert

By nightfall they reached the outskirts of the desert. Before them stretched a sandy region devoid of vegetation. Even the sparse brown bushes they passed on the steppe were gone. They found a small cave in a hill that would provide them shelter for the night. When the sun set, the temperature dropped dramatically. Chantel pulled her cloak tightly around her body as she sat at the cave entrance with Mouse, thinking about the next day, when they would enter the desert and with it the endlessness of the sand.

"I wish I had asked Owl more about the Warlord of the South," she said. "I wonder what he's like and where he lives. Are the screeching crows his allies?"

"I don't think so. The crows are from the mountains and thus would answer to the Warlord of the North, Aquila Bellum," Mouse replied. "But I wish I knew more about the South, too."

Suddenly Fox shouted from inside the cave, "Something lives here."

"What do you mean?" asked Mouse.

"See this fur?" said Fox. "Look at those paw prints. They look like a cat's."

"Cat!" Mouse jumped up. He peered at the prints on the cave floor.

Chantel almost laughed. "You have no reason to be frightened, Mouse. If I were a cat, I'd be terrified of the Mighty Warrior."

Mouse began to smile. "You're right. But where I was born, we were constantly attacked by sand cats."

"Perhaps this one was just passing through, like us," Chantel said.

"And perhaps it wasn't," added Fox.

"All the more reason for us to stay alert," Chantel said. "Who will take the first watch?"

"I will," Mouse said. "You two get some rest. If that cat comes back, I'll change into the Mighty Warrior and give it the scare of its life."

Mouse sat in front of the little cave and watched the red sun disappear behind the horizon. His ears twitched in all directions, but it was a quiet night.

He watched the moons rise. Even though he'd observed them many times before, the striking colors of the two moons still fascinated him. The blood red moon made him a little restless, while the silvery blue moon brought him peace, comfort and tranquility. He thought about the many times he had traveled the four lands alone, staying up late and watching the moons and appreciating all their beauty.

Although he liked traveling alone, he was happier traveling with Chantel and Fox. He couldn't imagine a life without Chantel anymore.

A sound startled him.

"Cat!" he yelped.

"No," said Fox. "It's just me."

"Already?" Mouse asked, astonished.

"Yes. Look at the two moons. Their nightly walk is at the halfway point."

"Time for me to get some rest, then. Good night, Fox."

Fox settled upside down, clinging to an overhanging rock at the cave mouth. He loved the night; it was his domain. In the distance he saw the sand dunes of the desert. The night winds played with the sand and moved the dunes from one place to another.

He missed Laluna a lot, even though he didn't show it during the day. But at night, when only the stars and the two moons were witnesses, lonely tears often dripped down his face.

He thought about the first time he'd met Laluna and how terrified and confused she'd been, stuck in the deep abyss. He remembered how painful it had been to have to show her the destroyed village of the Winged Ones.

Although he'd never admit it to Chantel or Mouse, Fox wished that he could fly to the Northwest to find the surviving Winged Ones rumored to live there with the wolves. When Laluna got better and returned, he wanted to be able to tell her that he'd seen them for himself. And he wanted to be able to tell her if any of her family members had survived and what exactly the wolves had meant.

"Time flies when you're lost in thought."

Chantel surprised Fox, who promptly flew down from his perch.

"Time already?" Fox asked.

"Time already," replied Chantel.

Chantel, wrapped in both her cloak and a blanket, sat on a rock outside the cave entrance. She tugged her hood firmly over her head and reassured herself that her Golden Braid was well hidden. She was surprised by how alert she felt despite having woken up only moments before. Her mind was clear; her senses sharp. She watched as the two moons completed their nightly travels and the horizon in the East started to glimmer with the light of the coming day. The fine line of orange that formed in the distance awoke a strange feeling in Chantel, and she thought about the events that had led up to the fight with the screeching crows.

"Orange is one of the missing colors that Fin didn't know about," she thought. "It is missing because it is connected to the Darkness, to the Evil One. But that doesn't mean I can't use it to help us. I need to learn how to use it better, this new power."

She sat cross-legged and took out the Magic Staff. "Orange," she thought. "The color of the rising sun. The hope for a new day."

The Staff's crystal lit up more quickly than she had expected, shimmering at first and then growing brighter and brighter. Chantel held her Staff tighter and felt the power pulsating through it. She felt drawn to it. She wanted to engulf it, accept it and feel it rushing through her body. Her braid weighed heavily from her head, the warning that something was wrong, but she ignored it as she gripped the Staff tighter and tighter. Then she was staring through bushes, through leaves. She was watching herself. Whose eyes was she looking through this time?

She blinked and came back to her own perspective. She lowered her Staff and bolted up. The orange light in the Staff's crystal immediately disappeared.

"Who are you? Who's there? Show yourself!"

Strangely enough, as she heard the crunching sound of paws on sand, her braid didn't grow heavier, which would have signaled a dangerous enemy. It grew lighter.

A small cat appeared slowly from behind a narrow sand hill. Her emerald eyes glittered in the early morning light. Her fur was light brown, almost the color of the sand, and her paws were broad so that she could move across the sand without sinking into it. Her tail was long with a black tip that twitched slightly.

"Who are you?" Chantel asked quietly.

"My name is Tac," purred the creature. "But more importantly, who are you?"

"I'm Chantel. I'm a wanderer." This was a lie that Chantel had used before, and it had always worked well.

But Tac wasn't satisfied. "You don't look like a wanderer, at least not like the wanderers of the desert. Etam Luos is a wanderer." Tac eyed Chantel carefully.

"What do you know about Etam Luos?"

Tac ignored the question and continued pacing in front of Chantel with her tail straight in the air.

"You keep strange company, wanderer. A Fox Bat and a mouse. The mouse would make a nice breakfast, but the bat is too leathery and too skinny."

"Don't be fooled by appearances," replied Chantel. "The mouse can put up a good fight." Then she repeated, "What do you know about Etam Luos? Do you know how to find him?"

Tac shook her head. "As I'd said, he's a true wanderer. You don't find wanderers. They find you. But since the coming of the Darkness, it's rare to see anyone, even the wanderers, roaming the desert. Many of the desert tribes are in hiding, afraid of the Sand Divers."

Chantel nodded. "It's hard times in all the lands," she added, thinking about the Mountain People hiding in their City of Ice under the Lake of Clouds.

"Yes," Tac replied. "But it's hardest in the desert. It always has been. There's little water and little food. The days are hot and the nights are cold."

Tac stopped pacing and stared at Chantel. "It may sound like I'm complaining but I'm not. I'm a sand cat; I love the desert. Before the Darkness, the desert was hostile, yes, but it was also the most liberating place of all the lands. You could run for miles in any direction. We danced with the falling stars during the half-moon times and sang the desert songs during the festival for the Midnight Blooming Cactus Flowers; and during special nights when all tribes united in the presence of the Spirit of the South, we felt complete.

But now it's different. Sand Divers are everywhere, killing every creature they come across to steal their food and water. You're lucky to have avoided them so far."

Tac gazed at Chantel's head. Then she leapt and swiped at Chantel's hood with her paw. Chantel tumbled off the rock.

"Hey!" cried Chantel. "What was that for?" She stood up, dusting herself off.

Tac's glittering green eyes were fixed on Chantel's hair.

"Ha! I thought so! I like your braid, Princess. It's as golden as the sand."

"My braid!" Chantel quickly pulled her hood back up.

"Don't worry. It is time that we meet. Eno Esiw, the Wise One of the South, sent me here. I've been waiting in this cave for you for many days already."

Chantel's angry expression melted away. "The Wise One of the South! I feared she was dead."

A look of pain passed through Tac's emerald eyes. "She's not, thank the Spirits, but . . ." Tac's voice trailed off. "We should begin our journey at once."

Chantel headed to the cave to wake Mouse and Fox, but they were already up, standing in the entrance. They had heard Chantel's outcry.

"Are you okay?" asked Fox, landing on Chantel's shoulder.

"I'm fine," said Chantel. "Meet our new friend, Tac."

"Friend?" Mouse's tail curled. He jumped onto Chantel's other shoulder. "Can I change and give her the scare of a lifetime?" he whispered.

"Don't you dare, Mouse," Chantel whispered back. "Tac's been sent by the Wise One."

"A Wise One who befriends cats?" muttered Mouse. "Great. Just great."

The three friends saw red clouds that lay heavily on the horizon in the East.

"Red clouds in the morning are a bad omen," Tac said. "The Wise One says that they didn't always foretell that, but they have for as long as I can remember. They always precede a day of battles and pain. We must move as quickly as possible. I don't want to face the Sand Divers."

"Where are we going?" Chantel asked.

"To Storm Mountain, a huge rock in the middle of the desert, the home of the Wise One. We will have to travel all day and half the night to reach it."

"If the red sky warning is real, don't you think we should hide today and travel during the night, when it's safer?" asked Mouse.

"Hide where?" said Tac scornfully. "Do you see any place to hide?"

Indeed, now that they'd entered the desert, there were no rocks or bushes at all—only miles of dunes and waves of sand.

"It was only a suggestion," muttered Mouse.

"Don't get your whiskers in a knot," said Tac.

"They're not."

"Really?" Tac grinned, showing off her sharp teeth. She wiggled her tail in Mouse's face.

"Stop it!" Mouse curled his paws into fists.

"You think you could fight me?" Tac purred.

"Would you prefer to be skinned or shredded?" Mouse challenged.

"Before you touch me, you'll be sliced into little pieces." Tac lifted her right paw, extending its sharp claws.

"Stop it!" Chantel cried, slamming her Staff between them. It sunk into the sand. "We've already got enough enemies. Can't you try to get along?"

"We'll finish this later, Mouse," snarled Tac. "We've got to move along quickly. I don't think the Sand Divers know we're here, but that could easily change. Only once we arrive at Storm Mountain will we be safe."

"What are the Sand Divers like?" Chantel asked, but Tac had already bounded forward, becoming a yellow speck quickly blending into the golden sand.

CHAPTER ELEVEN

The Sand Divers

The sun scorched down at midday. Chantel's yellow cloak reflected the hot rays, and its hood shaded her head. Fox and Mouse curled up in Chantel's inner pockets to stay cool. Chantel made sure they drank often from the bottomless water bottle. It was like sipping from a mountain stream; the water was so cold and refreshing. Tac politely declined every time Chantel offered her a drink. The sun and heat did not affect Tac. In fact, the hotter it got, the faster she moved, as if the sun's powerful rays gave her extra strength.

She stopped and put her right ear on the ground. She signaled to Chantel to stand still. Chantel felt a light vibration under her feet. The sand grains started to bounce on top of each other. Chantel looked around but she couldn't see anything. Her braid, however, grew very heavy, as if someone were pulling on it.

"Danger," whispered Chantel.

Her companions leapt into action. Fox wiggled out of Chantel's pocket and soared into the sky, scouting the area, while

Mouse jumped out and changed into the Mighty Warrior.

"What is it? What's wrong?" he bellowed to Tac.

Tac froze. She stared at Mouse in awe. "*Wow*. I . . . I didn't know . . . " she stammered.

The Mighty Warrior looked at her with his glittering eyes and gave her a smug smile that quickly changed back to a frown as the vibrations grew stronger.

"What's wrong?" he repeated.

Tac put her ear to the ground again but only for a moment.

"Sand Divers!" she exclaimed. "We've been discovered! Run!"

"Run where?" Chantel cried, gripping her Staff. "Where can we hide?"

"Follow me!" Tac cried as she sped across the sand.

Chantel and the Mighty Warrior chased after her. Fox flew overhead. In the distance, Chantel could see a group of rocks. "A hiding spot," she thought. As the vibrations in the ground became more and more violent, Chantel kept slipping and sinking. Tac, with her broad paws, had no problems running on the shifting sand.

Chantel felt a large paw around her waist, and she was lifted into the air. "Mouse!" she exclaimed.

"It's quicker this way," he said.

His broad feet moved easily across the sand, and soon they were nose-to-nose with the small sand cat. The Mighty Warrior picked Tac up and carried her, too.

Within moments, they reached the rocks. Fox landed on Chantel's shoulder. He was shaking.

"Did you see the Sand Divers?" she asked.

"There must be hundreds of them!" he exclaimed. "They rose out of the sand as if they were emerging from water. I've never seen anything like it. They move so quickly that the sand whirls around them. They will be here in a few minutes. I don't think these rocks will protect us."

"A hundred of them!" Tac looked shocked. "Yes, you're right, these rocks won't be enough." She stood on her hind legs and began to whistle.

Chantel looked across the desert and saw a huge sand cloud moving their way. The sand below the rocks rolled like a stormy sea. The Mighty Warrior drew his sword, and Chantel lifted her Magic Staff in front of her. For a second she thought about using her newly found sense to see what her enemy saw and think like her enemy did, but then she realized that it would be too dangerous to try new things when the enemy was so close. But the temptation was incredibly strong. The desire to know more played with Chantel's emotions, but she pointed the Staff at the sand cloud. "Indigo," she thought. "Winds will rise to help."

"What are you doing?" cried Tac.

"I am calling upon the winds. I did the same in the mountains when I fought the Snow Walker."

"Don't! If you create wind here, you'll unbalance the elements of the desert, which might create a vortex that would destroy us all. Wait! Help is coming!"

"Help? What help?"

"You'll see," said Tac, pacing the rocks. "I've whistled for them. They must be on their way."

Chantel continued to grip her Staff anyway. As she watched the sand cloud near, she was able to make out shapes in front of it: ugly creatures wearing glittering goggles, running, shouting and waving in anger. All of a sudden the creatures stopped. The sand around them settled and the ground stopped shaking.

Chantel could see the Sand Divers clearly. Their red eyes, enlarged by the goggles, were full of hatred. The rest of their faces were covered with white scarves, and their mouths were hidden behind black mouthpieces attached to shells fastened to their backs. Their hands were like shovels, perfectly shaped for digging, with sharp edges instead of fingers at the ends.

"Why did they stop?" Chantel wondered.

The sand in front of the rocks swirled like a whirlpool, and a man dressed in white rose up from its depths. He was twice the size of the others but, like the others, a white scarf covered his face and he breathed through a black tube. His eyes were red—redder than the blood red moon.

He ripped off his scarf and the tube and began to laugh loudly. His mouth was filled with sharp teeth as yellow as the sand.

The Sand Divers ripped off their scarves and tubes, too, and laughed with him.

"So this is the Princess of Freedom!" cried the man. "I thought she'd be a lot taller." His eyes traveled from Chantel to the Mighty Warrior to Fox to Tac and then back to Chantel.

"What a group of misfits." He turned to his Sand Divers. "Shall we crush them?"

They began to stomp their bare feet and yell. The man lifted his arm, and the stomping and yelling stopped. He turned back to Chantel and her friends.

"You heard my soldiers," he said. "I would have enjoyed your company, little Princess. Tormenting and torturing you would have brought me great pleasure. But unlike my counterpart in the North, I'd rather not waste time. What a fool Aquila Bellum must be to be frightened of you."

He tied his scarf back on and took another look at Chantel. He hesitated for a moment, seeing something in Chantel that reminded him of the Wise One of the South. "Young, innocent eyes," he thought. He shook his head, shaking off the memory, and as he repositioned his mouthpiece, he yelled, "GET HER!"

The ground began to shake again, and the Sand Divers rushed forward, slashing their shovel hands in the air.

"Your powers are our only hope now!" Tac yelled to Chantel. "The Storm Riders are too late!"

Chantel panicked. "I can't just call upon the power instantaneously. I need time to concentrate."

Tac arched her back and hissed. Chantel gulped and gripped her Staff and tried to focus, but her palms were slippery with sweat and the Staff kept slipping down.

The Sand Divers charged closer and closer.

"Focus! Focus!" she cried to herself. "Indigo!"

Tac continued to hiss and pace, which made Chantel panic even more.

The Mighty Warrior bowed down to her and said gently, "You can do it." His calm voice immediately had the desired effect on Chantel. "I believe in you."

Chantel took a deep breath and concentrated with all her might. Slowly the power grew inside her, and the Staff started to pulsate with an indigo color.

"Into my pocket! Quick!" she cried.

Mouse transformed back to his small self, and Fox dove down from the sky, burrowing himself into one of Chantel's cloak pockets. Tac leapt onto her shoulder.

Chantel raised her Magic Staff. The power raced through her veins, and she tried to imagine the hot winds of the desert blowing the Sand Divers away. But she hadn't given herself enough time to imagine what she wanted the power to do.

She raised the Staff, her arm shaking. The winds began to shriek as the first Sand Diver reached the rock formation. His sharp hand reached for her face, nearly slicing her cheek, before the powerful winds grabbed him and swept him and the others off their feet. He howled as the winds blew him and the others into the desert.

Chantel shook. The power was too strong. Losing her grip, she dropped the Staff, fainted and toppled off the rocks and onto the sand.

Tac jumped and landed on top of her. "Chantel! Chantel! Wake up! But don't open your eyes!"

Chantel moaned. She sat up, keeping her eyes closed. Her head felt dizzy and light. Sand beat against her skin and the wind howled.

"A vortex is coming!" Tac cried above the wind. "Keep your eyes closed. Hold on to the rocks for your life or you'll be blown away!"

With her eyes closed, Chantel felt around in the sand, found her Staff and tucked it into her belt. Then felt around blindly for the rocks. After a few moments of groping, she touched a clump and gripped them as tightly as she could. Tac clutched a big rock beside Chantel with her claws.

The unnatural wind that Chantel had called up had indeed offset the delicate balance of the desert's hot and cold cycles. The winds circled faster and faster, forming a massive funnel cloud. Within seconds, both Tac and Chantel, with Mouse and Fox hidden in Chantel's cloak, were torn from the rocks and sucked into the air.

The wind blasted the sand into Chantel's face. It felt like hundreds of needles poking at her eyelids at the same time. She tumbled head over heels and tried to cover her ears, but it was too late; they were already plugged with sand. Her nose was plugged, too. She could barely breathe. Then someone grabbed her. It felt like the Mighty Warrior gripping her around the waist, but it couldn't be him. Sand still beat against her face. She didn't dare open her eyes.

Something was pulled over her mouth and she was able to breathe again. She felt her feet touching the ground. Or was it the ground? Whatever she was standing on was moving up and down like a wave. Finally the movement became more and more gentle and the blasting sand settled.

Chantel cautiously opened her eyes. She and Tac were standing on a small disk that looked like it was made from silver sand. The disk, hovering above the ground, slowly moved forward. A man and a woman stood on either side of Chantel on the disk. Both were tall and dressed in tight yellow outfits. Scarves covered their faces and goggles like the ones the Sand Divers wore protected their eyes. But unlike the Sand Divers, friendly eyes with crinkles at their edges and gold flecks in their irises glinted behind the goggles' glass lenses.

Chantel watched as the woman pressed down her heels

and the man pressed down his toes and the disk gently rocked with the movements of their feet.

Around their wrists they wore leather bands with crisscrossing golden threads.

"That's the Storm Riders' emblem," Tac purred in her ear. She was sitting on Chantel's right shoulder now.

The ride continued for a few more minutes, and then the disk stopped moving forward and hovered a short distance above the ground.

"Come on," said Tac, leaping off.

Chantel jumped down. Her legs wobbled but she didn't tumble over. She turned around to thank the Storm Riders, but they'd already silently slipped away.

She shook her head. Sand crusted her hair and lined her nose and plugged her ears. It was even in her mouth and crunched between her teeth. Mouse and Fox climbed out of Chantel's cloak pocket. They were covered in sand, too.

"What happened?" Mouse asked, shaking his fur.

"Chantel's power created a vortex like I'd said it would," replied Tac. "We're lucky that the Storm Riders got there in time to help us."

"But you were the one that told me to use my power!" Chantel protested. "I saved us from the Sand Divers."

Tac looked humbled. "I was just hoping you would use some power other than wind. I . . . I'm sorry."

"It's okay. Without those two Storm Riders we would've all perished in the vortex. Who were they?" Chantel asked.

"They are members of one of the nomadic tribes of the desert. They live in the cliffs on the west side of Storm Mountain, away from the sun. The Warlord of the South and his helpers have tried for many moon crossings to capture them, but they can't reach them. The Storm Riders are too clever. The Storm Riders love sandstorms. I'm sure you will meet them again soon, and then you can thank them for rescuing us. Come on. We'd better get going. We've lost enough time thanks to Enim Ymene."

"So that was Enim, the Warlord of the South," said Chantel. "I thought so. What do you know about him?"

"I only know that he once was a leader of one of the nomadic desert tribes. He liked ruling over the Sand Divers, and he wanted to rule over all the other tribes as well. The Evil One promised him the Enchanted Medallion. If used for dark purposes, the Enchanted Medallion can create gold and silver or fulfill other desires. In the hands of one who is true at heart, it provides real wealth and shows the pathway to living simply and truly and being happy with what one already has. The Enchanted Medallion reinforces our existing values and beliefs."

"How come he was influenced by the Darkness?" Chantel wondered aloud.

"Because he lost touch with what is really valuable," Tac replied. "He believed that luxurious living would make him constantly happy. But that's a lie. No one can ever be constantly happy. Nor does happiness stem from getting more than what one needs. The Wise One will tell you more about this and the traditional beliefs and values of the South."

"You are full of wisdom, Tac," said Mouse.

Chantel nodded. "How long have you lived with the Wise One?"

"Since I was a little kitten," said Tac. "Eno saved me from the Sand Divers, and I have lived with her ever since. I have seen and heard many things. Some have taught me the power of simplicity, and some have showed me the folly of greed." Tac's tail twitched involuntarily.

"For instance?" Chantel asked gently.

Tac shook her head. "You will find out soon enough."

Chantel's braid grew heavy, and she knew that Tac was hiding something important, something that Tac didn't want to talk about, but rather than push her to reveal her secrets, Chantel and Mouse respected her silence and let her run ahead.

CHAPTER TWELVE

Many Evil Ones

Aquila Bellum made good time. He only rested when forced to by the darkness of the night, when clouds shrouded the two moons. He walked for five days straight with his lone wolverine trailing behind him. His few surviving winged informers, the screeching crows, had told him where Chantel was and he hurried to get there.

When he saw the funnel cloud far in the distance and heard the shrieks of battle, he knew that Enim had met Chantel. "Arrogant Enim has met her at last. I wonder how he's faring."

Aquila picked up his pace, watching the funnel cloud lose its strength until it vanished from the horizon.

Sensing excitement, his wolverine led the way with his nose in the air. Soon they came upon the defeated Sand Divers scattered over a large sand dune. Most of them were unconscious, half-sticking out of the sand like strange shrubs, with sand clotted over their wounds. In the center huddled a man rocking his head in his hands.

Aquila approached and towered above him.

"So you've met her, Enim?" Aquila Bellum tried to hide the satisfaction in his voice. "You look defeated, my friend. Would you like to tell me what happened?"

Enim Ymene raised his head. He scowled. "Wipe that smile off your face, Aquila. What are you doing here, anyway?"

"I came to kill the Princess. You didn't listen to my warning, so I knew you'd be in trouble. Chantel's no ordinary little girl. She's the Last Descendant, and her powers are growing. Soon she'll learn how to use the full potential of the Magic Staff. We must stop her before then. Get up and get your Sand Divers together. Don't give up so easily. Do you know where she's headed? Do you know the location of the Enchanted Medallion?"

"If I knew where it was, it would already be in my possession!" Enim cried.

"Well, at least have your spies and watchers track Chantel."

"I don't have spies or watchers. I have only my Sand Divers. This is the desert, a wasteland. Don't you know what that means? All we have here is sand, sand and more sand." Enim sat up. "Keep that wolverine away from me. I don't like the look in his eyes."

"He's hungry," said Aquila as the wolverine licked his lips and growled softly, "and so am I. Stop your whining. There must be a way to find her."

Enim sniffed. "The sandstorm has wiped away all their tracks."

"Tell me all you know about the surrounding desert,"

Aquila growled, stomping his foot. "And get up. You look terrible."

As Enim rose and shook the sand out of his clothes, he explained, "If you travel due south, you will reach Storm Mountain, where the Storm Riders live. We've tried to capture them, but it's proven impossible. They create strong shifting storms that protect the mountain against unwanted intruders. Some believe that Eno, the Wise One of the South, lives at the top of the mountain, but no one knows for sure. To the east lies the steppe where horse breeders and shepherds live. To the west live the Lost Ones. Nobody dares go there. The Lost Ones tried to withstand the calling of their dark side and failed to come to terms with it. No longer able to live with themselves, they went insane. Their constant struggle between good and bad transformed them in horrible ways. Some are physically deformed beyond recognition. Others have a disease that caused their skin to peel off and their bones to break easily. At night, when the wind is blowing in the right direction, you can hear their screams."

Enim grew silent. Long ago he had traveled into that terrible land and swore to himself that he would never go back there. He had tried to rescue his parents, who had resisted the calling of their dark side and had been transformed. When he had found them, he could hardly recognize them. Unable to bear looking into their lifeless eyes and listen to their constant howling, he turned away and ran. In nightmares he relived that horrible scene over and over again.

"That's all?" Aquila paced back and forth. His wolverine growled, sensing his master's irritation. "Tell me about the Medallion."

Enim Ymene's eyes lit up. "The Enchanted Medallion," he whispered. "He who holds it can change anyone into a slave. Can you imagine making the Wise One or even the leader of the desert tribes a slave?" Enim rubbed his hands as if it were already happening. "Once, eight moon crossings ago, when the Wise One of the South retrieved the Medallion from the castle, I almost got it, but she escaped with it. I don't know where she's hidden it."

"Useless," spat Aquila. He turned to the Sand Divers, who had clustered and were crouching around them. Behind their goggles their eyes glowed like red sparks, the same color as Aquila's. Aquila turned away from Enim to address them.

"Get up!" he cried. "Show me that you are a worthy army by catching Chantel, the Last Descendant, for the Evil One."

The Sand Divers leapt to their feet. They slashed their sharp shovel hands through the air in a salute. They'd heard rumors about the fierce Warlord of the North. He was the one who had awoken the Evil One. He was the Evil One's favorite warlord.

"They are my army now," thought Aquila, "and together we will destroy Chantel."

During the night, Aquila Bellum mentally scanned the desert, using his telepathic power to look for creatures that had turned to their dark side. "There have to be other evil ones," he thought. "Enim is just too weak to gather them together."

Aquila searched for the trademarks of the Darkness: greed and hatred. Sure enough, he soon located some of these creatures and telepathically contacted them. Due south he communicated with a group of Phaco Choerus (warthogs) that lived close to Storm Mountain. In the Southeast he connected with a family of Parahyaena Brunnea (brown hyena-like creatures). In the Southwest he recruited a herd of Lycaon Pictus (wild dogs).

Then Aquila concentrated even harder. He wanted all the evil ones in the desert—even the smallest of them, including spiders, snakes, and scorpions—to know about Chantel and the big hunt.

"Helpers of the Evil One, be aware," he mentally cried out to them. "The Last Descendant is in your desert land, searching for the Enchanted Medallion. She must not find it. She must be captured. The time has come for you to prove that you are worthy of the respect of the Evil One. Be on the lookout for the Golden Braid."

When he finished his telepathic summons and his mind relaxed, Aquila smirked. "This time, Princess, you will not escape me."

CHAPTER THIRTEEN

Storm Mountain

Once the sun set, the desert became cold and alive. Big and small creatures came out from their hiding places for their nightly hunt. Scorpions crawled through the sand, dust beetles awoke and jackals searched for rodents and insects. Night flowers opened up, and their colorful petals and leaves absorbed the desert dew that condensed in the cold of the night.

"It's not much farther to Storm Mountain, but I think we should stop and rest now and continue our journey tomorrow," Tac said.

"What about Enim and the Sand Divers?" asked Chantel.

"It'll take them a while to recover from that sandstorm."

After a quiet meal that consisted of the final bits of food that Owl had packed and lots of water from Chantel's bottle, they settled down for the night. The four travelers, wearied by the events of the day, quickly fell asleep huddled together to share their warmth.

When Chantel woke up, she was surprised to find Mouse still asleep. It was early, and the sand was covered with millions of tiny frosty star-shaped crystals. Chantel realized how cold she was. Shivering, she looked up towards the golden mountain that was now not too far away.

"Time to get up," she called out. All her companions were up in seconds. Chantel smiled proudly at the effect her voice had on them.

Once they'd collected all their belongings, they set off with Tac leading the way. The frosty sand crunched under their feet. Soon the sand warmed up, and traveling became more difficult. For every step forward up the slope towards the mountain, Chantel slid a half step back.

As the mountain neared, Chantel could see whirls of sand rushing around its base. She shuddered, thinking of the vortex.

"Don't worry," said Tac. "That storm isn't out of control. It's made by the Storm Riders who guard the mountain."

"But how are we supposed to get through it?" Mouse asked.

"Watch," said Tac. She curled her tongue and blew air through it. A high-pitched whistle escaped her mouth.

Chantel peered at the moving sand. Instead of swirling around and around, it was moving in waves around the mountain. Then out of the corner of her eye, she saw a silver glint. Storm Riders!

Three silver disks raced along the wave, which seemed to be coming straight at them. Mouse and Fox jumped into her pocket again, and Chantel covered her mouth and nose with her cloak and closed her eyes. Without warning, hands gripped her hips, and the Storm Riders lifted her into the air, setting her onto the solid disk. Sand pelted her skin as she felt the platform move up and down and back and forth beneath her. Then, as quickly as it had started, it stopped. Chantel felt herself being lifted off the disk and set down on the ground.

Chantel opened her eyes. She was standing at the base of Storm Mountain. She turned just in time to catch a glimpse of the departing Storm Riders, who waved as they disappeared back into their sea of sand.

Tac shook herself to get the sand out of her fur, and Mouse and Fox worked their way out of Chantel's sand-filled pockets.

"At the end of this quest I think I'll have eaten more sand than food," said Mouse.

"Complain, complain," muttered Tac. "Follow me," she said to Chantel.

Chantel looked with amazement at the sheer walls of Storm Mountain. They towered so high that she couldn't see the top. The rock face was golden and flawless, except for a few cracks that were mostly near the top and one larger crack at the base that was shaped like a lightning bolt. Tac stood in front of a narrow opening. "Through here," she said.

Tac slipped inside. Mouse and Fox followed easily, but Chantel had to squeeze through on her hands and knees. She spent a few tense moments crawling and feeling suffocated until the crack finally widened. She stood up, dusted her knees and stared into a vast, magnificent cavern lit by sunlight filtering through cracks in the overhanging walls.

The path that stretched out in front of her branched in many directions like the twisting roots of a tree. Each path was walled in with green bushes, hanging vines and many different colored flowers. Above the paths, the walls of the mountain leaned slightly inwards. On the sides, rocks jutted outwards, creating rocky ledges covered with sparkling flowers and moss. Trickling water fell from the cavern's ceiling. It was cool and beautiful. Chantel stared, overwhelmed by the colorful scenery and confused by all the walkways, the different levels inside the mountain and the diffused light. Little birds not much larger than dragonflies darted about everywhere. She felt as if she were immersed in an aquarium of life, protected from the rough elements of nature that surrounded the mountain.

"This is the beginning of the labyrinth of Storm Mountain," said Tac. "If you take the wrong path, you will be lost forever. So stay close to me. I've memorized the way that leads us to Eno. We have to get to that stairway over there." Tac pointed to the far wall where a stairway zigged and zagged around the ledges and led to the cavern's flat ceiling.

Chantel, Mouse and Fox followed Tac's lead through the labyrinth. It twisted and turned and often branched. Tac didn't hesitate. She always knew which way to go. After many twists and turns, they reached the staircase that scaled the mountain wall. Each stair was carved into stone and was very narrow.

"It's dangerous, but it's the only way to the top," said Tac, sensing their reluctance to go up the stairway.

At first Chantel wasn't afraid, but as she climbed higher and higher, she began to sweat. She hugged the wall and gripped the ledges. Fox flew beside Chantel to give her good advice.

"Don't look down," he said. "Always look forward, to the next step."

Chantel's arms and legs ached, and she was dusty and hot. Just as she thought she couldn't go any farther, she heard Tac call out, "We're here."

Chantel saw a round hole above her head. She gripped its edge and lifted herself through it, emerging at last at the top of Storm Mountain.

CHAPTER FOURTEEN

Making Plans

Although the Last Descendant will have known her guardian for many moon crossings, she will not know all, since she is only able to see what she is allowed to see. What goes on in the mind of others stays hidden, but never judge because of disappointment, since you do not know the whole story.

From The Book of Erebus

Owl circled the kitchen impatiently, wishing he could have told Chantel everything, wishing he didn't have to keep so many secrets from her.

Would the Evil One force him to take the Golden Sword from the castle? There was no way he could since the Golden Sword was hidden and protected by a spell Mother Nature had cast.

He heard a voice—a terrible voice—echoing in his head.

"Owl, old friend of the West, listen to me. You must get rid of that old fool, Fin. He doesn't serve any purpose anymore. Take him to the Endless Gorge and throw him into it. Nobody will ever find him."

"*Kill* Fin?" cried Owl. "But he's a Wise One!"

"Exactly," said the Evil One. "I can feel that the Darkness will not be with him much longer, so it's best to get rid of him now while he is weak. Do it, Owl. Do it now! It is my wish. I want my revenge."

"And when will it stop, Spirit?" asked Owl. "You've killed so many."

"There are more who need to be punished, especially the Mountain People. Only when all have felt the same pain I have will I be at peace."

"How can you ever be at peace again?" replied Owl, thinking to himself. "You're the one who killed the Winged Ones."

"Remember," the Evil One replied, "you took my side when you accompanied me and the soul of the last Spirit Bear to the afterworld, the world that is so far away from the spirit world, the world that I can't enter. You knew what I would do. You knew of my love and devotion to those special creatures. Now, get rid of that old Wise One. Don't try my patience. Be careful, Owl, or you will find the same end as your precious Winged Ones."

CHAPTER FIFTEEN

Eno Esiw

As the Last Descendant travels the four lands and meets with the past, she will mature and claim her powers and abilities. The Wise Ones will teach and guide her. The stronger she becomes, the less the prophecy and the truth that comes with it will harm the bearer of the Golden Braid.

From The Book of Erebus

The view from the top of Storm Mountain was breathtaking. Chantel felt like she could touch the sky. Even though the sun was close, a brisk wind that swept across the large flat space made it much cooler than it was on the desert dunes below. Several trees grew in a circle around an eight-sided tent. The light yellow color of the tent blended in with the sandy ground. The trees' bark was a light yellow color, too, but the trees' leaves were a bright, lush, healthy-looking green.

Tac ran ahead and vanished behind a brown flap that covered the tent's entrance. Chantel was unsure of what to do. Did Tac expect them to follow her?

Just as Chantel took a few steps forward, a voice called from within the tent, "Come in, Princess. It is time for us to meet."

Chantel ducked under the flap. Mouse and Fox followed.

A beautiful woman seated on pillows on the floor in the middle of the tent greeted them with a smile. She was wearing a simple dark yellow sundress that complemented her tanned skin. Long black hair fell over her shoulders. It looked dry and brittle. Her eyes were large and green like Tac's, but unlike Tac's, they were flat and lifeless, like the glass eyes of a doll.

Unnerved, Chantel averted her gaze. There was very little furniture in the tent. There was a colorful handwoven rug with small hills of bright pillows. In one corner, several glasses and a pitcher of golden liquid sat on a low table. In another corner, a hammock swung gently between two wooden posts. The light that came through the tent's dome was soft and warm.

Tac swung in the hammock, her tail moving back and forth like a pendulum. A brown curtain near the hammock fluttered, leading to another room.

"I sense someone in the other room," Fox whispered into Chantel's ear as he landed on her shoulder.

"Yes, I do, too," murmured Chantel.

"Something familiar," added Fox. "Something good." He felt excited and nervous, though he wasn't sure why.

The woman's voice interrupted their whisperings.

"Please find a pillow and take a seat. I am Eno, the Wise One of the South. Welcome to my home."

As Chantel picked a pillow and sat down, Eno rose and offered her a cup of lemonade, which Chantel accepted thankfully. The lemonade was delicious, sweet and cool. Eno poured some of it into a dish near the door flap. Mouse, thinking it was for him, hopped over to take a sip, and Fox flew down and landed next to him.

"That's my dish," Tac hissed from the hammock before they could take a drink.

Eno turned around and chided, "Tac, these are our guests. We have invited them into our tent, and we share our food with them."

Chantel watched the slender woman and thought about her new sense. "Maybe I can try to slip into Eno's mind and see what she is hiding and why she looks so tired." Her fingers twitched nervously. She didn't really know how to do it. She didn't even know if there were particular words that went along with the spell. Her inner voice warned her, "You are playing with the Evil One's power. You can't just invade another person's privacy whenever you want to."

Chantel blushed. "But if I knew what was wrong I could help," Chantel argued with herself.

Eno turned her flat green eyes to Chantel again. "I'm glad you're here. There is something I must attend to now, but we will have time to speak tomorrow. Make yourself comfortable and use the pillows to sleep on. You will find no need for sheets. This tent is made from a special material that retains the heat of the day." Eno slipped behind the curtain that divided the tent and returned a few seconds later with a plate of grapes and bread. "As for food, I hope this will satisfy you. It is too late to start another fire."

"This is fine. Thank you, Wise One," replied Chantel, ashamed of her previous thoughts.

"Please call me Eno," she said. "Good night."

With that, Eno disappeared behind the curtain again with Tac at her heels. Chantel, Fox and Mouse were alone.

"What do you think?" Chantel whispered to her friends.

"Something's wrong," whispered Mouse.

"Someone else is here," added Fox.

"And Eno is hiding a secret," continued Mouse.

"Do you think she's hiding the Enchanted Medallion up here somewhere?" whispered Chantel.

"No, I don't think so. I think it's something else," Mouse whispered back.

They ate the grapes in silence, thinking about the same people: Fin and Eno. They knew that even the Wise Ones weren't immune to the Darkness. When they finished their food, they stacked their glasses on top of the empty plate and put it in the corner.

"Now you should get some rest, Chantel," said Mouse. "I'll keep watch," he added, "just in case."

CHAPTER SIXTEEN

Getting Closer

Aquila Bellum was up early that morning and walked around the camp of the Sand Divers.

"Pitiful," he thought.

Most of the Sand Divers were lying on the ground, sleeping wherever they had fallen down the previous night. Enim's tent was the only shelter, and even it looked pathetic. It was pitched crookedly, and its fabric was faded and torn in several places. One of Enim's legs stuck out of the tent opening.

"You fools will never capture Chantel," Aquila said.

Slowly life came into the camp. One by one the Sand Divers woke up. As soon as they opened their eyes, they were hungry. Some dove into the sand, seeking the succulent sandworms that lived deep below the surface. Others got their bows and arrows and left to hunt desert rabbits and sand cats.

"Well, at least they don't waste any time once they're awake," Aquila thought.

By midmorning the Sand Divers were satiated and milling around. As Aquila recruited them to go after the Princess of

Freedom, he noticed a sand cloud moving towards them. He pulled out his sword and waited. Within a few minutes two warthogs arrived.

"Are you the Snow Walker?" they asked.

"Yes," he said.

"We have news for you. A wall of sand ate a girl, a sand cat, a mouse and a Fox Bat near Storm Mountain."

"Chantel!" Aquila knew that it would be a waste of time to try to enter Storm Mountain because the protective storms would not allow him to even get close to that rock, but he could make sure that he camped out nearby. Eventually Chantel would have to leave the mountain, and when she did, he'd be ready for her.

Aquila jerked on Enim's leg. "Wake up! Chantel is on Storm Mountain. I will need ten of your strongest Sand Divers to accompany me."

"Wha . . ." Enim stammered groggily, poking his head out of the tent.

"I know where Chantel is, and I am going to get her."

"You do? Where is she?"

"She's at the top of Storm Mountain. She must be meeting with the Wise One there."

"So it's true: our Wise One lives at the top of the mountain."

"What do you mean, *our* Wise One? She's our enemy!"

Enim's eyes, however, had glazed over. "We used to be friends . . . before . . . I wonder if she's okay, after what I did to her . . . "

"You're a weakling, Enim!" cried Aquila. "No warlord should ever think about such things! Now let's go! GO!"

"Yes, Aquila," Enim squeaked, slinking away like a sandworm.

The minute he was gone, Aquila put his hand on his chest where the white lightning bolt had hit him. The scar ached.

Aquila growled, "Perhaps I should get rid of Enim. Perhaps I should feed him to my wolverine." Hearing this, the wolverine, sweating in the sun, nodded and wetted his lips with his long purple tongue. "Be patient. Not today," Aquila said to his companion. "He is still useful for now."

Aquila's small army of Sand Divers packed quickly and was ready to go. The night had just begun, and only the silvery blue moon shimmered in the sky. Aquila preferred to travel by the light of the blood red moon.

Silvery blue or blood red, Aquila was glad to be leaving Enim. Enim had constantly complained as he did the simple task of organizing the Sand Divers who were to accompany Aquila.

"It's not as easy for me as it is for you," Enim had whined. "I have no hyenas or wolverines to help."

And when he wasn't whining, Enim continued to dwell on thoughts about Eno, telling Aquila how her screams still haunted his dreams.

Aquila had taken his wolverine aside. "Stay here and watch Enim for me," Aquila had said. "If he does something stupid, eat him."

With that, Aquila and his army began their trek to Storm Mountain. They marched on and on. The Sand Divers, not accustomed to a long journey, began to whine and complain much like Enim did.

Finally Aquila could take it no longer. Even though Storm Mountain was still far away, they set up camp early behind a cluster of red and orange rocks that looked like a giant petrified fire.

As Aquila lay down to sleep, he gave his mind an order. "I command you! Do not dream!" But his mind did not obey orders as faithfully as his beasts did, and as soon as he was asleep, the dreams he had forbidden began. He dreamt about his sister, Procella, whom his father had always called "little rose." He dreamt that he rescued her from the river's freezing waters. He wrapped her in his warm jacket and rubbed her hair and face dry. When she opened her eyes and looked up at him, it wasn't Procella who gazed into his eyes; it was Chantel!

CHAPTER SEVENTEEN

Another Winged One

Chantel woke up to a delicious smell. She quickly dressed and left the tent, following her nose. Although the sun had already risen, it was still chilly outside.

Eno, shaded by five trees, stood several meters away from the tent in front of a small oven made of clay. Pots and pans lay scattered on the ground. Chantel's growling stomach gave her away.

"Hungry?" the Wise One asked without turning around.

"Yes. What are you making?"

"Vegetable flat bread," replied Eno. "It's the most practical food in the land of the South because it can be made with the most basic ingredients: flour and seeds, garlic, and then whatever vegetables are available, like tomato, cactus leaves, sand flowers or zucchini. The Storm Riders are kind enough to supply me with what I need. I once tried to grow tomatoes, garlic and zucchini, but the nights up here are too cold; with the frost and constant wind, all my attempts failed. The Storm Riders grow their vegetables within Storm Mountain, where the temperatures are mild and no cold breezes blow. Storm Mountain's life power comes from within. A mystical being lives in its heart and emanates the ancient strength of balance."

Eno opened the oven door. A small fire continued to glow below the chamber where loaves of thin bread baked. Eno shut the oven door. "A few more moments and it will be ready."

Chantel's stomach growled again. To distract it, she gazed at the view. The swirling sands of the storms whipped around the mountain's base. Chantel felt that she and her friends were truly protected. Was Eno hiding up here from Enim and his Sand Divers? Or was she hiding from something else? Why was Eno being so secretive?

Chantel looked at Eno with questioning eyes.

"I will explain later, Princess. I promise," said Eno, sensing what Chantel was thinking. "For now, all I can tell you is that I am afraid—afraid of what is coming and afraid of my memories—memories of what the evil ones did to me. Please be patient."

Eno opened the oven door again. "It's ready." She carefully removed the thin loaves and placed them in a basket. "Come. Let's share this with the others."

Inside the tent, Mouse, Fox and Tac were already sitting up, perched on pillows on the floor.

"Mmm . . . that smells good," said Mouse. "I'm so hungry."

Tac and Fox were eager to eat, too. Just as Eno was about to divide the food, the curtain parted and a young boy appeared.

Chantel stared at the boy with shock. Poking above his shoulders were the tips of two brown wings. He was no normal boy—he was a Winged One!

"So the wolves were right!" thought Chantel, her heart pounding. The sudden appearance of the boy left her speechless.

"You must be feeling better," greeted Eno.

"I am. Thank you," replied the boy. His voice, however, sounded tired.

"Please join us for breakfast," Eno said, gesturing to a pillow.

The Winged One approached the group, and as he neared, Chantel got a better look at him. His face was soft but reddish colored, as though he were recovering from a terrible sunburn. His hair was thick and brown like his wings. In many ways he looked like Laluna. He bowed before Chantel.

"It is my pleasure to meet you, Princess," he said politely. "My name is Ilsole. Eno told me about you last night. I was too ill too get up, but I feel much better today."

"You should still be resting," Eno said. She turned to Chantel. "Ilsole is a Winged One from the West. He is one of the last of his kind, one of the few who survived the attack of the Evil One. Four nights ago, he landed on my mountain. Dehydrated and exhausted, he was nearly dead."

"Without you, Eno, I surely would be dead," added Ilsole.

Eno smiled and handed him the basket of bread. Then she found a cushion to sit on, and Chantel did the same. As they shared their breakfast, Chantel and Fox kept staring at Ilsole.

"Is there something you wish to ask me?" Ilsole finally murmured.

Chantel blushed and looked down at her rune stone. "Sorry. I didn't mean to be so rude. It's just that you remind me of my friend Laluna, who is also a Winged One. We thought she was the last Winged One alive."

"Laluna?" Ilsole choked on his bread and coughed. "Laluna!" he cried, jumping up. "So it's true! She's still alive!"

"Be calm, Ilsole," said Eno.

Ilsole sat down, coughing, his eyes burning with excitement. "Where is she? How do you know her?"

"I met Laluna on my journey into the mountains of the North to recover the Golden Sword," Chantel explained. "She rescued me from attacking Vampire Bats. We became very good friends. We became sisters."

"She offered you sisterhood? That is a rare thing for a Winged One to do. She must have trusted you very much. What happened to her? Why isn't she with you now?" Ilsole's eyes glittered with excitement and an unexplained happiness.

"She was injured during a fight," Chantel said, her smile quickly disappearing and her eyes filling with tears. "She's somewhere underground in the land of the North, close to the mountains and the waterfall. Mother Nature is caring for her."

"I must go to her," said Ilsole. "She's the reason I'm here. All the Winged Ones who survived the red lightning bolt have been taking refuge with the wolves in the West. Those who survived were either away hunting or traveling during the attack. When the red lightning bolt struck, I was with a group of ten Young Ones on a field trip with an elder. Now I have been sent on a special search to find Laluna. We were hoping that she would still be alive, but we weren't sure.

All the others are too frightened to leave and search. The red lightning bolt that exploded not too long ago haunts their dreams." He shuddered. "Mine, too."

Chantel gulped. "I have released that red lightning bolt. I felt such hate towards the beast that was attacking Laluna and such love for Laluna at the same time that a red lightning bolt sprung from my Magic Staff."

"You released the red lightning bolt?" Ilsole replied in disbelief. "It takes great strength to be able to do that without being killed."

"It almost did kill me. My Soul Mate, Etam Luos, saved me. He made sure the hate didn't overwhelm me. He kept me mindful of love."

Now it was Eno's turn to look shocked. "Etam Luos? He's your Soul Mate?"

Chantel described her vision. "Do you know him, Eno?"

"Yes, I know him. I know him very well. We were once great friends." She noticed Ilsole pocketing his bread. "What are you doing?"

"I must go to Laluna at once," he said.

"Not yet. You must fully heal. You're not ready to travel yet, especially alone."

"And Laluna needs to heal, too," added Chantel. "But you're welcome to come with us when we return to the North. I'm sure that Mother Nature will let you see her then."

"Thank you," said Ilsole. "There is so much that I have to tell her."

CHAPTER EIGHTEEN

Healing

Laluna hobbled in a circle. Every day she took a few more steps. It seemed to her that more animals with bandages and injuries were lying in Mother Nature's cave. In one corner lay a little deer with her left leg bandaged. A yellow candle burned beside her. Across from Laluna was a badger. His head and chest were bandaged, and a green candle burned beside him.

"It feels like I've been here for a long time," she thought.

"Up and walking already?" Mother Nature observed. She looked tired. The leaves that made up her dress were dry and some were cracked. The strain of healing all the injured creatures was taking its toll on her.

"A few more steps every day," Laluna replied. "I want to return to Chantel as soon as I can. But it's still hard for me to move. How long have I been here, Mother Nature?"

"I'm not sure. When I'm down in my cave, I sometimes forget about time. It's easy to lose track of it when you don't see the daily phases of the sun and moons."

"I hope Chantel is okay," Laluna said. "Mother Nature, I've been thinking . . . "

"Yes?"

"Why did the Solenodon attack me instead of Chantel? The Solenodon was headed for Chantel, but then it swerved and landed on me. Why?"

"I think you should know, Laluna, that you have probably guessed correctly. It's a long story, and I have sworn to keep part of it secret. But it's true: the Solenodon surely meant to kill you. Without you, it knew that Chantel would not be able to complete her quest."

"Mother Nature . . . " a weak voice called from a far corner of the cave. It belonged to a small rabbit whose front right leg was bandaged.

"I will be back soon, Laluna," said Mother Nature.

As Mother Nature walked towards the rabbit, Laluna sat down on her moss bed, feeling very dizzy, very afraid and very lonely.

CHAPTER NINETEEN

Attempted Murder

Fin woke up. He didn't know where he was, who he was or what had happened. His head pounded. He tried to remember, but the harder he tried, the worse his headache became. His mind was clouded with an impenetrable fog. All he could remember was a flash of red light and a girl with a Golden Braid.

It was pitch black. Fin tried to move, but his arms and legs were tightly bound. He heard footsteps. A door creaked open and a beam of light shot through his prison. Before he could see who had opened the door, a cold liquid was thrown into his face and eyes, blinding him.

There was a great flapping sound, and something sharp grabbed his shoulders, ripping his shirt and jabbing his skin. The pain was so intense that he fainted and descended into complete darkness.

Owl flew high into the sky with Fin's numb body dangling from his claws. As he flew, he murmured the tune of worship to the Spirit of the West.

After a few hours of flight, Owl turned his head and opened his claws just above the Endless Gorge.

"Sorry," he whispered. Without looking down, he flew back to the castle.

Fin fell down, down, down.

A great gray hand shot out from the side of the cliff.

THUMP!

"Gotcha!" exclaimed the Rock Climber.

When Fin woke up, it was the middle of the night. He couldn't move, nor could he see, and not just because it was dark. The liquid that had been flung in his eyes burned so badly that he was afraid to open them. When he tried to move, it felt as if all the bones in his body were broken. His shirt stuck to his shoulders with dried blood. He fainted again.

The next time he awoke, the pain was still intense, and when he finally opened his eyes, he could only see shadows and lights. He couldn't make out any details of his surroundings, but he was happy that he wasn't completely blind.

"Anybody here?" he yelled.

"Yes," a deep voice answered.

"Who are you?" Fin's voice trembled.

"I am the one who caught you. I am a Rock Climber. I can help you."

"Thank you," Fin said. He couldn't remember if Rock Climbers were friends or foes. "Can you please tell me where I am?" he asked, concerned.

"Yes. You're on the northern edge of the Endless Gorge. Whoever dropped you really wanted to get rid of you, Wise One."

"You know me?"

"Yes. Your name is Eronimus Finsh. You live up in the mountain, near the waterfall."

"I remember," Fin whispered. "I remember my cave and the view from the mountain plateau. Eronimus Finsh. Yes. That is my name. Will you untie me, please?"

"Turn around," said the Rock Climber.

Fin felt stone-cold hands touching him, and the ropes that held him slowly fell off.

"Are you able to get up?" the Rock Climber asked.

"I think I can if you help me."

With the Rock Climber's rock-solid hand supporting him, Fin slowly rose to his feet.

"I will help you to your cave," the Rock Climber said. "Don't forget your feather," he added, crawling clumsily over the edge of the cliff and onto solid ground.

"What feather?" asked Fin.

"The one you had in your hand when I caught you. The one beside your right foot."

Fin bent down and felt the ground until he felt something soft. He picked it up. "Is this it?" he asked, only seeing a long narrow-shaped object in his hand. His vision was very blurry.

"Yes."

Fin put it in his cloak pocket. He felt that it was important to find out what it was.

Large rock hands lifted Fin from the ground. Fin groaned in pain.

"Sorry," the Rock Climber said.

"It's . . . it's all right. Thank you," Fin mumbled through clenched teeth.

Holding Fin as gently as he could, the Rock Climber began to walk slowly and unsteadily, shifting from one side to the other.

"Rock Climbers usually don't leave the cliffs," he said, "but I smell that you are good. And I smell Chantel on you. She is my special friend."

"Chantel, yes," Fin thought and he became excited. "Brave little girl. I hope she is doing well. I wonder where she is now."

After an hour of stumbling step taking, the Rock Climber finally reached the plateau. He carefully put Fin on the ground and helped him up. Fin was able to stand, but he moved as awkwardly as the Rock Climber did. The waterfall was near. Fin could feel the fresh mist on his face and hear the roaring water ringing in his ears.

"Thank you again, Rock Climber," Fin called out.

"You're welcome, Wise One of the North. Good-bye."

Fin maneuvered behind the layers of water that tumbled

down from above to find the entrance to his cave. He walked slowly and carefully. Although his eyes could only differentiate between black and white and everything was blurry, he made his way to his cave entrance.

As he entered, he stumbled over broken furniture and gagged on a putrid smell.

"What happened here?" Fin wondered in dismay, visualizing what it looked like. He felt his way along the wall to the ladder that led to the next level of his cave. After finding his shelves across the hidden window, he felt around and brought some odd vessels close to his eyes until he found the one he was looking for.

Fin opened it and used his index finger to extract some of the cream and rubbed it on his eyelids. The cold feeling on his eyes gave him hope and peace. He felt for his bed and found it quickly. As soon as his body touched the soft mattress, he was asleep.

The night was peaceful, and the two moons looked over the mountain plateau, engulfing it in a mysterious light. Fin's dreams, however, were not peaceful. Dark creatures with long knifelike claws were chasing him, ripping his cloth and piercing his skin.

CHAPTER TWENTY

The Inner Light

After they had finished eating breakfast, Eno took Chantel outside.

"So Etam Luos is your Soul Mate," Eno said, her dull eyes gazing out across the sand dunes. "It finally makes sense. Etam Luos has always had two names here in the desert. One of them, Lla Fo Dneirf, means Friend of All. That name made sense, for he cares for all the tribes. But his other name, Etam Luos, Soul Mate, never made sense to me until now."

"What do you mean, his name is Soul Mate?" asked Chantel.

"All the names of the South are simple," explained Eno. "They tell who we are, only in reverse, like Tac—Cat —or Enim Ymene—Enemy Mine. But everyone is and has a Soul Mate, so I never understood why Lla Fo Dneirf was named the Soul Mate. I assumed it was because he was everyone's Soul Mate, just as he was everyone's friend. But now I understand: he is the Soul Mate of the Princess of Freedom and thus the Soul Mate of Freedom, a very important Soul Mate indeed.

"I owe Lla Fo Dneirf my life," Eno went on. "He rescued me from the Sand Divers eight moon crossings ago. We lost contact after that. But it's vital that you find him, for reasons besides him being your Soul Mate. As guardian of the tribes, he holds the Key to finding the Enchanted Medallion."

"The Key to the Enchanted Medallion!" exclaimed Chantel. "Do you know where the Enchanted Medallion is?"

"The Medallion is hidden in Storm Mountain's labyrinth. I can show you where to start the search, but you will never find the Medallion without Etam's Key."

"I have to find him at once."

"Go where?" replied Eno. "Wander the desert aimlessly? No. You must wait here for a sign from him."

"Maybe I can contact him in my mind," said Chantel. "I was able to do it before."

Chantel stared out at the still, golden desert. She closed her eyes and concentrated. "Etam!" she thought. "Etam!" There was no response. She opened her eyes again.

"Any luck?" asked Eno, who was now sitting cross-legged on the ground.

Chantel sat down, shaking her head. "Why can't I find him? Why won't he come to me?"

"When I grow frustrated, I meditate," said Eno. "It is through meditation that you will be able to use the colors of the Staff without the Staff itself."

"I don't understand."

"Tac told me about the Sand Divers and how you fainted from using your Staff's power. I have good news for you: You may think that the Staff holds power, but really it doesn't. You're the one with the power, and one day you'll be strong enough to release the power without the help of the Magic Staff. Right now the Staff functions as a channeling device. Without it guiding your power, your power would have already destroyed you. But once you've mastered the ability to see and understand your Inner Light, you will be able to know when your powers are growing too strong and threaten to destroy you, or when they are too weak and you're in danger of losing your soul."

"My Inner Light?" asked Chantel.

"Yes. Your Inner Light is a flame inside you that represents your soul's strength. When you are weak, it burns faintly. When you are strong, it burns brightly."

"But how can I see it if it's inside me?"

"I've developed a way of meditation that allows one to get in contact with one's Inner Light," replied Eno. "You have to be perfectly at peace with yourself. Would you like to try?"

"Yes, please," said Chantel.

"Good. Close your eyes and try to relax completely. Forget all your worries and all your fears. Concentrate on your body. Start with your toes and visualize yourself crawling up your body towards your head."

Chantel tried her best. The sun was very hot and sweat ran down her face. She focused on her feet, and they began to tingle. Slowly the muscles in her toes and feet started to relax. Then she focused on her legs. Again she felt a tingling sensation, and slowly the muscles in her legs relaxed. Next were her lower body, followed by her arms and her upper body, and finally the feeling of relaxation reached her head.

"Once you're completely relaxed, you can focus on your mental feelings like anxiety, love and fear," Eno intoned.

"And after you have relaxed and released those feelings, you will be able to feel your true self in its simplest form. Then you will be able to see your Inner Light," Eno whispered into Chantel's ear, "the little light inside of you. Its shine will show you the way back if you are lost. That's your Inner Light."

Chantel focused and concentrated. Finally both her body and her mind were completely relaxed. Then she turned her thoughts inwards. And that's when she saw it. A small light appeared in the surrounding darkness. It flickered faintly, glowing in the color of magenta.

"I see it! Eno, I see it!"

"You do?" Eno's voice was filled with joy and a strange urgency. "Tell me, what is it like? Describe it to me!"

But Chantel didn't get a chance. Eno's voice drifted away.

Chantel watched as her Inner Light burst into a thousand tiny sparkles, revealing none other than Etam Luos floating in the air right in front of her face.

"I'm sorry I couldn't come when you called. The desert is swarming with evil ones. Someone is calling on them," he said.

"Where are you?" Chantel asked.

"I'm in a far corner of the desert, visiting the forgotten ones who wander the planes without direction and purpose. But I'm moving tonight. In two days, take your water bottle, your Magic Staff and your cloak and start walking due south. You must come alone so that none of your friends will have to face the same consequences we will have to face."

"What 'consequences'?"

"When I came to you in the vision and you released the

red lightning bolt, the Evil One didn't only sense you; she also sensed me. She might be able to contact us very easily when we are together, and who knows what she may do then? There is something I must give you; otherwise I wouldn't ask you to come to me." Etam was suddenly quiet.

"The Key to the Enchanted Medallion," Chantel said.

"Yes . . . the Key . . . " Etam's voice faded into a tune, which also quickly faded away.

"So Etam Luos came in a vision to save me and thereby endangered himself," Chantel thought, opening her eyes at last. "And in two days I will finally meet him."

CHAPTER TWENTY-ONE

New Friendships

Chantel spent the rest of the day with Eno, practicing finding her Inner Light, and using her Magic Staff at the same time. When Chantel focused on her Inner Light she could call on six of the Staff's seven colors, including red and orange. She still couldn't call on violet. She didn't know what the meaning of violet was and what it could do, but she remembered Fin's warning that it, like red and orange, was the color of the Evil One. Using her powers, Chantel built fires and walls, created waterfalls and windstorms, and made Eno float in the sky and the clay oven disappear. She was tempted again to use the orange color to find out more about Eno's past, but she controlled her urge and restrained herself. She also didn't dare call on red, remembering the terrible consequences of the red lightning bolt.

While Chantel and Eno spent their day together, Ilsole and Fox soared in the sky high above Storm Mountain. Fox told Ilsole all about Laluna and how she had grown up in his tribe of Fox Bats. Ilsole listened quietly.

"How do you feel?" Fox asked him after they had landed on the mountain plateau.

"I think the flight was a little too long. I should rest now, but I'd like to tell you my story."

Fox followed Ilsole into the tent. Ilsole lay down on a hammock while Fox perched on a pillow.

"The few of us who survived were not in the village when the red lightning bolt destroyed it," Ilsole began. "I was with a group of young Winged Ones looking for mushrooms and clay. The others were hunting or fishing. We didn't know what had happened; all we saw was a red light and we heard a loud explosion. I couldn't see for a while—the light was so bright. The ground shook and we were knocked down.

"When the wolves found us, we were all afraid and in shock, hiding in the forest surrounding our village. We followed the wolves deeper into the mountains and forest of the West, where we slowly recovered. Some of us went back to our destroyed village and looked for more survivors, but we didn't find any. They recovered a few of the ancient books in the destroyed library. I read them all, and I found out about the Circle of Four. Laluna is part of it and so am I, and two other young Winged Ones, Lanotte and Ilgiorno. Laluna means moon; Lanotte means night; Ilsole means sun, and Ilgiorno means day. Our duty is to help stop the Evil One from returning to the four lands."

"But I thought Chantel was responsible for that," replied Fox. "I thought that all the relics, when they are brought together, will release enough light power to banish the Darkness for good. How are you supposed to help?"

"The prophecy states that when the Evil One returns, it will first destroy our village. Then four young Winged Ones must take four magic stones and place them in a circle around the Evil One. The power of the stones will temporarily hold the Evil One, trapping it as if in a spider's web. Hopefully they will hold the Evil One long enough for Chantel to recover all four relics and release the light power. But without Laluna, it is impossible to make that circle. I'm glad that you found and rescued her, friend Fox," said Ilsole quietly as he drifted into sleep.

"Me, too," Fox thought, seeing Laluna's face appear in his mind.

Meanwhile, Mouse and Tac were left together on the north side of the mountain plateau, staring at each other in silence. Despite all they had been through together, the silence between them was tense.

"Your kind has killed members of my family," Mouse finally said.

"This is part of our nature," replied Tac. "You are part of our food source. What do you want to do? Change into the Mighty Warrior and squash me to get revenge?"

"Chantel wouldn't like that. Chantel is right. We have bigger enemies to battle."

"What do you mean?"

"You know the desert, and you know our enemies, the Sand Divers. And having a common enemy unites."

Tac looked at Mouse with questioning eyes, but she understood.

"The Sand Divers killed my family. Eno rescued me. Since then we have fought them many times."

"I have fought Vampire Bats, wolverines, hyenas and the Snow Walker," Mouse said, changing into the Mighty Warrior. "See here?" he pointed at the right side of his big head. "This scar is from the Snow Walker's sword." He removed the armor from his right shoulder. "And here is where the teeth of his wolverine punctured my skin."

Tac smiled.

"What?" the Mighty Warrior asked, slightly irritated.

"That is nothing," Tac replied. She moved the fur above her right ear aside and showed the Might Warrior a long scar that ran from her ear to her eye. "I got this in an encounter with four night crawlers, vicious creatures with yellow eyes and long claws. Even though I was blinded by my own blood, I killed them all!"

"Ha!" protested the Might Warrior. He pointed to his knee where a red line moved along his upper leg. "A spear, thrown by a crazy human, went right through my leg here. I broke the spear in half to pull it out of my leg. I have never been in so much pain since!"

"That is only physical pain," Tac said seriously. "Mental pain can be worse. I know."

Mouse was about to argue but noticed a deep sadness in Tac's purr. "What do you mean?"

Tac began, "Eight moon crossings ago, Eno was tortured by Enim. He killed three of her best friends right in front of her eyes. Eno has never fully recovered from that. She blames herself for the death of her friends. As a result, the worst thing that can happen to anyone happened to her: her Inner Light went out, extinguished by her tears."

"So that is what's wrong with her," said Mouse.

"But I've noticed," added Tac, "that she has been more cheerful since Chantel arrived. Maybe the Princess can help her."

"Chantel is a great Princess," replied Mouse. "If anyone can find a way, she will."

As the day came to an end, everyone gathered at the western edge of Storm Mountain, eating flat bread and sipping lemonade, to watch the sunset. The sky was a mix of colors: yellow, orange and red, and above the red there was a faint magenta glow. The wind played with the desert sand, building hills and valleys.

Chantel pointed to the magenta light in the sky. "That's the color of my Inner Light, Eno."

Eno gazed up at the purple-red beams. For once her flat eyes seemed to catch a little sparkle. "Magenta is a strong, harmonious color," she said.

The sparkle in Eno's eyes turned into tears that dripped down her cheeks, leaving her eyes flat and dull again.

Ilsole, who was also gazing at the sunset, began to chant softly:

Trapa raf dna tnereffid erew yeht ecno
Straeh ynam yb devol erew htob tub
Emit hguorht dnob a yb detcennoc
Enim eb lliw dna eno era yeht won

"What did you just say?" Chantel asked.

"It's an old saying I read about in the ancient books of the Winged Ones. I always chant it when I see a sunset like this. It is somehow connected to the Evil One. It is said that the Evil One colors the sky orange, violet and red to remind us that she will return."

"I've heard the chant before, too," Chantel said. "Do you know what it means?"

"I don't," Ilsole replied, "except that it is a warning. None of the Winged Ones' books of wisdom translated it; they all said that one has to read *The Book of Erebus* to find the translation and the complete history of the four lands and the truth."

"Do you know where that book is?" asked Chantel.

"The Forest People are its keepers. At least that's what I've been told."

They all went to bed after the moons had taken over the sky. The blood red one was traveling behind the silvery blue one—a good sign that heralds a few peaceful days ahead.

It was cool inside the tent, and soon it was filled with the sound of slow, even breathing—the sound of sleep. Only Mouse and Chantel lay awake. Mouse crouched beside Chantel's pillow.

"Tac told me what happened to Eno. And now I'll tell you," Mouse whispered to her.

As Chantel listened, tears filled her eyes, and when Mouse was done, a dangerous thought entered her mind: she must use her newfound power to find out how Eno felt without her Inner Light and see if there was any way she could help her.

When Mouse was asleep, Chantel picked up her Staff and headed outside the tent. Once again, Chantel's braid hung heavily and pulled at her skull, and once again she ignored it. She concentrated and began to meditate. The orange light began to shine in her Staff's crystal. She gripped the Staff tightly. The power filled her slowly, and she began to wander in the darkness of her mind. She searched for something—a clue, a hint of how to locate Eno. Several lights lit up in the distance, and it was as if Chantel was looking through many endless tubes to find what she was looking for. She focused on one that called out to her. It was as if she heard Eno's voice traveling through it.

She saw Ilsole in front of her. At first she didn't understand why he was there, but then she realized that she was looking at Ilsole through Eno's eyes.

Chantel had made it!

She turned her thoughts inwards, and a terrible feeling overcame her. Panic rose in her, and she felt lonely, so very lonely. And then she was utterly afraid, floating in nothing but darkness. She felt like she was drowning. She couldn't breathe.

Despite this feeling, Chantel looked deeper into Eno's thoughts and into Eno's memory. "Why? Why?" she whispered. "How did this happen? Show me."

Then she was running through the desert. Tac was by her side now, along with three young women.

Chantel realized that she was Eno Esiw, and the three young women were Eno's best friends from the horse breeder tribe.

"Hurry!" cried one of the women.

"Get them! Now!" shouted Enim Ymene, running after them. Sand Divers burst from the sand in front of them. They had been waiting in ambush. Eno and her group fell backwards. Within moments the Sand Divers had bound Eno's hands and feet. "Where is the Medallion hidden? Tell us!" the Sand Divers demanded, but Eno refused to answer.

The Sand Divers took one of Eno's best friends and dragged her below the sand. "Tell us where it's hidden!" demanded the Sand Divers.

"Don't tell them!" cried Eno's friend as she sunk deeper and deeper into the sand. Eno closed her eyes.

Her friend finally suffocated in the sand. The Sand Divers took Eno's next friend and then the last one and did it again. As each one was drowning beneath the sand, Eno's tears fell harder, mixing with the sand the Sand Divers threw in her face. Eno screamed in anger and frustration, in hatred and disgust, but the Sand Divers didn't stop.

Enim Ymene stood beside Eno through it all, watching her and whispering into her ear. "Give it up, Eno. You will be next. It is not worth dying for that thing. Give me the Enchanted Medallion and you will live, Eno Esiw."

He kept talking and talking, but Eno just shook her head. Enim would kill her whether or not she told him where the Medallion was hidden. As her tears kept coming, they began to not only drown her eyes and face but they also began to fill up her insides until her Inner Light was extinguished. She felt dark, hollow and hopeless.

When the last one of her friends was dead, Enim turned to her. He hissed into her ear, "Give it up! For the last time, where is the Enchanted Medallion?"

Eno still shook her head.

"She is yours," Enim yelled to his Sand Divers. The Sand Divers came running. Some started to kick her sides; others threw sand in her face until she collapsed into unconsciousness.

With everybody focusing on their helpless victim, they did not notice the wall of sand racing towards them and within it the army of Storm Riders.

Tac was the only one who had escaped the ambush. Enim hadn't sent a Sand Diver after the cat because he didn't think capturing her was important. Tac, however, would have been a most worthwhile catch since she was carrying the Enchanted Medallion in a pouch on her back. Tac had found Etam Luos and the Storm Riders, and they hurried to rescue the Wise One of the South.

When Eno opened her eyes again, she was lying in the canyon of Storm Mountain. Tac was sleeping beside her, still wearing the pouch. Eno reached for it and held it gently. She heard a calm, quiet voice call out to her. The sound traveled with the warm wind that was constantly blowing through the many paths that led through the base of Storm Mountain. She followed the voice for hours, lost within the labyrinth, before finally reaching a leafless tree.

"Place the Enchanted Medallion on one of my branches,"

the tree said. "I am the last one of the ancient ones from the desert, and I have been waiting for the return of our sacred relic. Once you have given up the Medallion, only the Last Descendant will be able to retrieve it."

Just as Eno reached into the pouch, Chantel left Eno's memories in the Wise One's mind and returned to herself. She took a deep breath. Her heart was pounding, and she still felt like she was in Eno's body. She couldn't feel her Inner Light. Chantel began to panic. Was her Inner Light extinguished by the tears she had cried for Eno and for Eno's friends? Then she felt a faint flicker and sighed with relief.

"Chantel," she heard through a thick fog. "Chantel." The voice was louder this time.

"Chantel, what have you done?" Eno shouted. She stood beside Chantel. Her hands were formed into fists and her whole body trembled. "You used the dark power on me. How dare you invade my privacy? How could you bring back all those memories I have been trying to forget all these years?" Tears streamed down Eno's face.

"I . . . I just wanted to help," Chantel stammered.

"You are closer to the Evil One than you are to me. How dare you?"

Eno turned around and stormed back into the tent, leaving Chantel alone with her Staff and her shame.

CHAPTER TWENTY-TWO

Redemption

The next day on Storm Mountain was one of the longest days in Chantel's life. While Mouse and Tac traded fighting techniques and Fox and Ilsole shared memories of the Winged Ones, Chantel practiced meditating with Eno. Eno didn't mention anything about the previous night, but she was short-tempered and barely spoke. Chantel tried to address her intrusion and how badly she felt about it, but Eno didn't want to hear anything about it.

"You are here for the greater good, and that is all. Don't expect anything else from me," Eno said coldly and closed her eyes.

Finally the day ended. Before they went to sleep, they had a small evening snack and watched the two moons appear in the North. Nobody said a word. Mouse, Fox and Tac all sensed the tension between the Princess and the Wise One.

In the middle of the night, a strange sound filtered in from outside the tent and woke Chantel. She rolled off her pillow, making sure not to squish Mouse or step on Tac's tail, and tiptoed outside.

Eno sat at the southern edge of the mountaintop, humming a song and crying at the same time. Chantel sat down next to her.

"I am so very sorry, Eno," Chantel began. "Please forgive me."

Eno turned and looked at Chantel with sad, empty eyes.

"I am trying to decide," said Eno.

"Decide what?" Chantel asked.

"I am not sure if you really meant well or if you were overcome by greed and curiosity to use your newfound power on me. I am trying to decide whether or not I can ever trust you again."

Chantel hung her head. "I wanted to help, but I was afraid to ask you," she whispered.

Eno looked into the distance at something that couldn't be seen, something that was lost in her thoughts and inner pain.

"Fear is dangerous. It is a driving force of the Darkness. The pain and fear of death I have experienced makes me hide inside. I have been running away from life. I'm a worthless Wise One."

"You *are* a Wise One," Chantel said. "You've put aside your pain to teach me. You are stronger than you think, Eno. Come. Let's meditate together for a while and find some peace."

Eno nodded. They held hands and began to concentrate. Soon they were moving through space in their minds.

Then they both heard a strange voice that sounded like

leaves rubbing against each other when the wind blows through a willow tree.

"Follow me," the voice said.

"It can't be," whispered Eno. "I know that voice! It's the voice of the Spirit of the South!"

A small bright yellow ball of light danced in front of them. Together Chantel and Eno followed the light through the air. Below them the desert disappeared and a great body of water came into view. They landed side by side on the shore of a vast ocean. Waves pounded the shore and mist filled the air. Through the mist, floating across the water, humanlike creatures slowly approached them. The creatures were faceless and their bodies transparent. They wore cloaks made of seaweed.

"The Spirit of the South, the yellow light you followed, guided you to us," they said in voices filled with various clicks and whistles. "She's been feeling your pain for some time now, Eno Esiw, Wise One of the South, and she has finally decided to help you."

"Who are you?" asked Chantel, leaning forward. She still could not see their faces, but she could make out friendly dark eyes set in bluish gray skin. For a moment she thought one of them had a long thin beak, but when she looked again the beak was gone.

"We are the Growers of the West, where water meets land and where rainbows originate," the creatures said. "We are the ones who grew your Magic Staff, Princess of Freedom. One day, when you are ready to travel into our land, the land of the West, you'll meet us and see us fully, but for now, listen closely. Do you know what you can do with the yellow color and the Staff?"

"Yes," Chantel said. She recited the ancient writings, "'Fire: Craving heat and warmth? Wrap yourself in blankets.' If I think yellow, I can create fire."

"Correct. We also know about another one of your powers—the new one, the dangerous one, the Evil One's. We feel your desire to use it, but if you do so without guidance, you will get closer to the Evil One every time you use this power. It is dangerous and careless undertaking on your part."

Chantel felt tension and shame creep up her body as she remembered what she had done the previous night.

"Don't be tempted again to use something you can't control. Giving in to temptation only leads to disaster. Don't use something that is not meant for you to use," the creatures warned her. Then they continued, "But there is a way you can help. Use the power of yellow to relight Eno's Inner Light. Focus again like you did when you closed the door to Fin's mind."

"But I've never used the yellow light on a human being," Chantel said, trembling. "I might light Eno on fire. I might kill her!"

The Growers shook their heads. "This is the only way, Princess."

"But . . . "

"You can do it, Chantel," said Eno. "I believe in your powers. Please try. I never thought I'd ever get my Inner Light back."

"But . . . I don't have my Staff," Chantel protested.

"You won't need it this time," replied the Growers. "We will guide you. Concentrate. You can do it."

Chantel took a deep breath and thought about the color yellow. She thought about the sand and the sun's yellow rays.

"The sun gives life and can also take it away. Good, Chantel," praised the Growers. Their voices sounded like waves crossing an endless ocean and rolling onto a sandy shore.

The power grew stronger and the image of the sun grew brighter in Chantel's mind. She looked deep into Eno's lifeless eyes and felt as if she were drawn right into them. She floated into darkness and was surrounded by emptiness. It was the same feeling she had experienced before.

"Now release the power and let the yellow light go," said the Growers.

Chantel did as she was bid. A bright yellow light moved away from her and into the darkness. For a brief moment, Chantel was standing in a large hall engulfed in a warm bright shine. Then once again she was standing in front of Eno, gazing into her eyes.

Eno took a deep, wobbly breath. She staggered and shook violently but caught herself just before falling down. Chantel saw a yellow flame burning behind Eno's eyes.

"It's done," the Growers said. "Chantel, you truly are the Last Descendant, but don't give in to temptation. Even the Last Descendent can be weak at times and drawn into the Darkness. Stay strong. We will be waiting for you."

Chantel and Eno were back on Storm Mountain. Whether or not they had actually left the mountaintop, they didn't know. Eno gazed at Chantel. Her green eyes danced.

"Your eyes! They're alive!" cried Chantel.

"My Inner Light . . . it's burning again. You did it, Chantel. You lit it!" Tears streamed down Eno's cheeks. "Thank you, Princess."

Chantel stood up and gave Eno a long hug. They were engulfed in the red light of the sun rising above the land of the East. Eno's face shone as brightly as the yellow morning flowers.

"Let's prepare breakfast together again before you leave," Eno said, full of energy and hope.

"Leave? Of course!" Chantel remembered. "Today I must meet Etam!"

CHAPTER TWENTY-THREE

An Unbelievable Thought

What was once unbelievable became reality. Time changes everything. Even the most stable values, ideas and traditions will be affected by the continuous change. What stays with us and gives us strength is hope, the desire to believe that everything will end well, but most of us lose our empathy because we are closest only to ourselves.

From The Book of Erebus

Fin woke up with a pounding headache. His eyes had stopped burning, but he was afraid to open them. What if his herbs hadn't worked? What if everything was still dim and blurry?

"Who blinded me?" he wondered. "Who took me from the castle and dropped me into the Gorge to kill me? If only Chantel hadn't closed my mind! If only I hadn't been locked up in a dungeon!" He began to grow angry, but then he remembered the anger and jealousy he had felt and how badly he had acted. He knew that Chantel had been right to close his mind. Still, he wondered how he had ended up being dropped into the Gorge.

"A creature of the Darkness must've snuck into the castle . . . It is no longer safe. I have to warn Chantel. She will be walking right into danger when she returns from her quest."

Fin was determined to find out exactly what had happened. He opened his eyes, no longer afraid for himself. To his great relief, he could see. His herbs had worked their magic. His vision wasn't perfect; everything was slightly blurry, but it was better than before, when he could only see shadows. After a while, his vision began to clear completely. He saw his shelves filled with colorful vials, he saw the end of his bed, and he saw the window that was hidden from the outside.

Fin got out of bed, walked to the window, and looked out at the beautiful green valley and the snow-covered mountain peaks. Each step caused him much pain, but he was overjoyed at being able to see again.

"I'm home," he said happily.

He turned around and hobbled downstairs. His cave was completely disheveled. The furniture was broken, his kitchen was in ruins, and an awful smell—like the aroma of the stinking manure-flower that grew beside small muddy ponds—filled the air. He walked around in disbelief and anger.

"Who did this?" he wondered. He sat beside his cold fireplace and held his head in his hands.

"At least I am still alive," he thought. A smile crossed his face when he thought about brave Chantel and friendly Laluna. With renewed energy and hope, he got up and started to clean his cave dwelling when he noticed a long gray feather on the ground.

"What is this?" he said as he bent down to pick it up. He remembered the Rock Climber who had reminded him to take it with him. He turned it over and let it slide through his fingers. Panic filled his eyes as he realized whom the feather belonged to.

"It can't be! I don't believe it! It doesn't make any sense!" He stared at the feather. "What should I do? I am too weak to face Owl. I could ask the Rock Climbers for help, but it will take them weeks to reach the castle." Then he exclaimed, "Aurora! She will help! She can send soldiers to the castle and capture Owl!"

He began to pace around his cave. "I have to find Aurora and the Mountain People. Chantel is in great danger and doesn't know it. Aurora will help. She has to."

He grabbed his cloak and old walking stick and hobbled out of his cave and through the waterfall. Pain brought tears to his eyes, but he forced himself to keep moving forward as he traveled the same path Chantel had taken when she first walked into the mountain world.

CHAPTER TWENTY-FOUR

Finding
Etam Luos

Trapa raf dna tnereffid erew yeht ecno
Straeh ynam yb devol erew htob tub
Emit hguorht dnob nommoc a yb detcennoc
Enim eb lliw dna eno era yeht won

Who knows what this means? The Last
Descendant has to find out; the answer is
the key to the Evil One's heart. One knows,
but will he be willing to share his knowledge?
But first the Last Descendent has to face
herself.

                    From The Book of Erebus

Immediately after breakfast, Chantel gathered her things and descended Storm Mountain's steep stairs. It didn't take her as long to walk down them as it had to climb up. When she reached the entrance of the mountain, the Storm Riders picked her up and carried her through the protective storms and let her down on the southern side. Chantel shook the sand out of her hair and ears. She dumped the sand out of the hood of her cloak and pulled it over her head.

Alone and ready to meet Etam, Chantel marched due south. The golden sand of the desert was soft, and she sank up to her ankles with every step she took.

"This is going to be a tough journey," she thought.

"Yes, it will be," she heard Etam say, "but there is no other way."

"Where can I find you?" Chantel exclaimed in her mind.

"Not where but when—whenever you are ready," said Etam.

"What do you mean?" Chantel asked.

"To find me, you must realize something. But I can't tell you what it is. I can only give you a clue. You blame yourself for what happened to Laluna. You have to learn that things happen in life, and some are out of your control. We have to accept what has happened, learn from it and move on."

"But I am supposed to be where Laluna is right now. I should be the one in Mother Nature's cave."

"Are you sure?"

"Please explain," Chantel's mind inquired.

"There are two possibilities," replied Etam. "One, Laluna is just as important as you are in fulfilling the quest, and the Evil One wanted to get rid of her. Or two, the Evil One wanted to harm someone you loved to hurt you."

"Why?"

"You must know by now that there are worse hurts than physical ones."

Chantel remembered Eno. The loss of Eno's friends had caused her Inner Light to die out. Chantel understood that feeling. If Laluna were to die . . . Chantel held up her rune stone to the North. Again, its flicker was dull.

Focusing on the rune stone, Chantel didn't notice a stone in the sand. She stumbled and fell to the ground. Her Golden Braid came out from under her hood.

A small scorpion looking for some shade from the burning sun saw her fall. "Too big for a light midday snack," he thought. His eyes weren't very good and he was old and slow, but he still could see something hanging down from the girl's head.

"The Golden Braid—the sign of the Last Descendant," the scorpion yelled with excitement. "I have to tell the Warlord of the North."

Aquila Bellum was delighted when he heard the scorpion's news.

"Chantel has left Storm Mountain! And she is only a two-day march away from me!" he said triumphantly. He notified his Sand Divers, who were diving in the sand looking for juicy, spicy Fire Leaches.

"Time to go!" he commanded.

Instead of marching, Aquila ran, and the Sand Divers had a hard time keeping up. After they had been running for a while, one of the Sand Divers whined, "Wait up! Can't we take a break now? I'm hungry and tired."

Aquila stopped but didn't turn around.

"So you are hungry?" A wicked smile crossed Aquila's face.

"Yes," groaned the Sand Diver. "We're all hungry. We left before we had found enough breakfast!"

"So you want to hunt worms and leaches instead of the Princess?"

"Yes. We are not your sla . . . "

The Sand Diver didn't have a chance to finish. Aquila grabbed him by the throat and broke his neck with one hand. Then Aquila lifted him up over his head and threw him onto the sand. The Sand Diver's lifeless body landed with a soft thump.

"Anybody else hungry? I can stop that feeling for you right away," he hissed.

All the other Sand Divers were perfectly silent; a soft, warm breeze touched their skin. They could still hear the crunching sound of their friend's snapping neck.

Aquila turned around and started to run. He was excited. He enjoyed the hunt, and he looked forward to catching his prey.

"This time I will kill you, Princess of Freedom," Aquila thought, his dark side stronger than ever, "and then I'll never dream of you again!"

The remaining Sand Divers quickly followed him without any words of complaint.

Chantel got back on her feet and took a drink from her water bottle.

"Etam?" she called out in her mind. But she was alone now. Etam's two possibilities circled in her mind.

"It doesn't make sense that the Evil One would want to hurt but not kill me. Even if she does like tormenting people, it is in her best interest to just kill me."

Her mind was distressed by these thoughts and by being alone, without anyone to talk to. As she continued to walk, her emotions welled up. The sun was burning down on her and sweat ran down her back. She thought about her Soul Mate and couldn't wait until he spoke to her again.

"Etam," she whispered again.

"Hello, Princess," a voice replied.

Chantel was terrified. She knew that voice. She'd heard it before, and she hated it.

"I can always feel and hear you when your emotions are high and you worry."

"Leave me alone, Evil One," Chantel thought.

"I can't. You are too important. One day you will understand me. You will feel the loneliness and hopelessness I feel, almost like the way the Wise One of the South felt without her Inner Light . . . but worse. You know that feeling. Remember?"

Chantel had no choice but to listen. She shivered, thinking about how Eno had felt and how emotionally empty she had been.

"I don't want to kill you; you must know that," the dark voice continued. "I need you, but I can't tell my warlords that or they would lose faith in me. Find your Soul Mate and listen and learn. You and I will meet one day, face-to-face, after you have learned the truth. By the way, how do you like my present?"

"What present?" Chantel asked.

"The one that tempts you so much. The one that awoke your greed for more. The orange color."

The voice was gone. Chantel was frightened. She knew that the Evil One was referring to her new sense. She tried to focus and tried to get rid of her dark thoughts.

"I have to focus on Etam and what he meant," Chantel thought. Her feet automatically moved forward. She cleared her mind and thought about her friends. "So the Evil One wants me to feel lonely and hopeless, so perhaps she is trying to kill those I love, but also . . . " Chantel remembered what Ilsole had said, about how Laluna was part of the circle of Young Ones. "Laluna is needed to stop the Evil One, too, so . . . perhaps it is both. This quest is not only about me. Everyone has to do his or her part. We all are in this together, and each of us has an essential role to play."

Her pace quickened. She felt stronger and in control again.

"Etam," she said confidently. "I know now. Can you hear me?"

Chantel listened but there was no answer.

"Where are you? I know now what you meant. I am not alone. I can't save the four lands by myself. Everyone has to be involved. Etam!"

"I am right here," a voice beside her said. Chantel started to smile. She knew that comforting voice, and this time it was not just in her head. She looked to her right and saw the smiling eyes of the figure in her vision. Etam Luos looked younger in person. His skin was light brown like Eno's, and his eyes were a sparkling grayish green. His pants, shirt and headband were all light yellow, and he wore light brown leather boots. His hair color matched his clothing.

"Etam Luos," whispered Chantel. "Soul Mate."

"Yes, you've found me," Etam said with a smile.

Without even trying to sense it, Chantel could feel her Inner Light blaze with strength.

"Come into my tent. It's cooler and more comfortable in there."

Chantel saw a yellow tent in front of her. "Where did that come from?" she wondered.

Without questioning, she followed Etam. Like Eno's tent, this one had eight corners, but unlike Eno's, it was bare except for two pillows and two blankets.

"Welcome to my home."

"Thank you," said Chantel.

She felt awkward and unsure of what to do, but she didn't need to think. Etam held up his hand, and Chantel instinctively reached up to touch his fingertips. Small blue lightning bolts crisscrossed between them until they were completely engulfed in a bluish light. A series of visions began to flash in front of Chantel's eyes.

A young Etam swaddled in blankets, abandoned in the desert and discovered by Mother Nature.

A young Etam living with Mother Nature in her cave, learning how to magically move from place to place quicker than the blink of an eye.

An older Etam leaving Mother Nature and returning to the land of the South.

A desert festival, where Etam played a flute and a gorgeous woman dressed in yellow danced nearby.

And finally the present-aged Etam, playing on his flute in the middle of the night while desert creatures danced around his tent.

When the blue light faded away, both Chantel and Etam collapsed onto the ground.

"I didn't know. I never would have guessed," they both said at the same time, looking at each other.

"All . . . all the pain you have experienced is . . . overwhelming," stammered Etam.

"My pain?"

"Laluna, Fin, your battles with Aquila, the Sand Divers . . . your mother . . . "

"What about my mother?" Chantel asked.

"I saw her giving birth to you. I saw her die. A white light filled the cave. I . . . "

Chantel's eyes widened in horror. "Die! That's impossible! My mother is alive. I know she is! I've seen her face guiding me."

"I don't know. Perhaps I saw wrong."

Etam looked horrified as he saw Chantel's disappointment. "The vision I saw ended with a great bright light. Maybe something happened and she didn't really die."

Etam Luos held out his hand, and Chantel touched her fingertips to his again. Her fingers shook. This time, red sparks crossed between them. Chantel's sadness slowly disappeared as her body filled with warmth.

After sharing a dinner of roasted lizard, cactus meat and sandworm pudding, Etam pulled out a small golden flute from his shirt pocket and started to play. Beautiful music filled the tent.

"Are you going to play for the desert creatures tonight?" asked Chantel. "Can I join you?"

"How do you know I do that?" said Etam, surprised.

"I had visions of you, too."

"I would love for you to join me. Lie down now and get some rest. I will wake you when it is dark and the night creatures come out."

During her short rest, Chantel dreamt about white creatures surrounding her and looking down at her. They were talking, but Chantel could not understand what they were saying. It was in a language that was strange to her. She could not see their faces. Then one of the creatures bent down, and Chantel saw the beautiful face of a young woman. She had long brown hair with a braid on one side. Her skin was soft and smooth. The woman gave Chantel a kiss. "I am alive. Find me, my Chantel," the woman said, "but I am not as you imagine."

"Time to wake up, Chantel," said Etam.

Chantel got up and walked outside the tent, where Etam sat cross-legged on a small rug. Chantel sat down beside him.

The two moons were already high in the sky. The silvery blue moon shone especially bright. The air was cold, and

Chantel was glad she had her warm cloak. Etam took out his small flute and began to play.

After a while, Chantel noticed some movement below the sand. Etam stopped playing.

A family of Sand Swimmers appeared. They had big eyes that were covered with a white protective film that they could move aside when they were not swimming in the sand and needed to see. Their bodies were smooth and long, almost like snakes but wider. Gray scales covered their heads.

"Etam, we need your advice," one of the Sand Swimmers said. "Little Squid here always complains about everything, no matter what we get him."

"But . . ." Little Squid complained.

"See? What did I just say? We get him delicious food, treats and toys like sand marbles and dew string, which are really hard to find, yet he's never happy."

"But I don't want them," Little Squid protested.

This continued for a while until Etam finally raised his arms and everybody listened.

"I think you have to return to what you believe in, which is simplicity," he said to the Sand Swimmer. "Your problem is that you don't listen. You mean well when you get things for Little Squid, but have you ever asked him what he really wants?"

The swimmers looked at each other, unable to say a word. They realized what they had done. Finally the eldest of the Sand Swimmers admitted, "You're right, Etam. What do you really want, Little Squid?"

Little Squid swam over and gave his elder a hug, "I just want to play with you."

The elder returned the hug and said, "And that's what you will get, Little Squid."

"Thank you, Etam and friend of Etam," the Sand Swimmer family said before they disappeared below the sand.

Etam began to play his flute again.

The ground started to vibrate, and Chantel heard loud pounding sounds coming closer very quickly. Two yellow Desert Runners stood in front of them. They looked like a cross between lizards and large wingless birds. A long red tongue came out of their sharp beaks periodically. They stood on two massive legs and were at least as tall as the Mighty Warrior.

"We need your help, Etam," one of them hissed. "We keep running into each other when we are hunting together. What can we do?"

Etam smiled and replied, "When you are hunting together, run side by side and not towards each other. This way the prey you chase will remain in front of you and will not escape, and you'll avoid hitting each other, too."

"We will do that. Great idea! Thank you," they hissed as they turned around and ran away.

"How did you know the answer so quickly?" Chantel asked.

"This is the third time I have seen those two. They always have the same problem. They're not the brightest of the desert creatures," explained Etam.

Chantel and Etam laughed. Then Etam handed Chantel the golden flute.

"Your turn," he said.

As Chantel learned to play the flute, the area around them

became alive with all sorts of night creatures. Dune Sliders skated across the sand. Storm Chasers danced in whirling circles. Slow Cave Diggers swayed to the music, letting tiny Sand Ants crawl on their backs, while the Desert Salamanders just lay still, listening to the music with their eyes closed. No one was thinking about the Sand Divers or the Darkness or the Evil One. Everyone and everything was peaceful. Even the silvery moon seemed to sway with the music.

A yellow light appeared behind Etam and Chantel—the same yellow light that had shown Chantel and Eno the way to the Growers.

"You play very well, Princess."

Chantel stopped playing and turned around. All the creatures fell silent and bowed their heads.

It was the Spirit of the South, floating inches above the sand. She was a tall woman, wearing a sheer dress that looked like it had been formed from sunbeams. In the center of her chest blazed a pulsing yellow light. Her face was pale except for her eyes, which shone like topaz.

"Thank you for helping the Wise One of the South find her way again," she said. "I'm on my way to reconnect with her, but I wanted to talk to you first. My brothers and I have decided that it is time to return to the four lands. But it is up to the creatures, humans and especially you, Chantel, to bring back peace. To do so, there is something you must know, something I must tell you, something that is very painful for me to admit." She paused and then said clearly, "The Spirit of the West, my spirit sister, is the Evil One."

All the desert creatures gasped. Etam looked at Chantel. She was stunned.

"Your sister?"

The Spirit of the South hushed them and continued, "My two brothers and I banished our sister after the Great War. Only Mother Nature, the Wise One of the West and the spirits know this. Mother Nature swore an oath to us three spirits to keep secret the identity of the Evil One. That's why she hasn't told you. When your friend Laluna was injured, Mother Nature contacted us spirits, pleading for our help. Her passion swayed our minds, but I was still skeptical about keeping the truth from you. Then when I saw what you had done for the Wise One of my land, I decided to tell you the truth. The spirits and the Wise Ones are Soul Mates, connecting the spirit world with your world. We spirits are very attached to our Wise Ones.

"When you are strong enough, Chantel, you will find out about your ancestry and the reason why you are called the Last Descendant and why the Spirit of the West turned evil. For now, believe in yourself and continue with your quest. All will make sense in time."

"The Evil One is the Spirit of the West," Chantel repeated. "My enemy is a spirit. How can I defeat a spirit?"

"You cannot," said the Spirit of the South.

"But . . . "

The Spirit of the South looked hesitant. Finally she said, "You can release her."

"But how?"

"I can't say any more. My brothers resent me telling you anything about our sister."

"I understand, but please answer one more question. Who is the Wise One of the West? If the spirits and the Wise

Ones are Soul Mates, then the Wise One of the West must also be connected with the Evil One."

"Since my sister destroyed the village of the Winged Ones, I haven't seen the Wise One of the West. At that time he was a small white owl."

"A white owl?" repeated Chantel.

"Yes," said the spirit. "I must go now. I have been here too long already, but I will continue to watch and see if there are ways I can help. Keep on playing the songs of the desert. They give us all strength."

With those words, she dimmed away completely.

Chantel continued to play the flute until the moons disappeared in the East and the night creatures started to seek shade. "Come. Let's go inside the tent now," said Etam. "We must get some rest before the sun begins to shine."

"Your flute," said Chantel, handing it back to Etam. But he wouldn't take it.

"Keep it safe," he said. "It is the Key to finding the Enchanted Medallion."

"*This* is the Key? The flute? But how?"

"I will explain how it works in the morning," said Etam. "Good night, Chantel."

Chantel hung the flute around her neck. The leather cord attached to the flute was soft and the flute itself felt warm against Chantel's chest.

Chantel's dreams came slowly. First they were pleasant. She was standing on the top of her tower, staring out at the northern mountains. She saw a small white bird flying high in the sky. It circled the castle gracefully. Chantel watched the bird's marvelous flight. All of a sudden, it turned and dove.

It flew closer and closer very quickly, and as it approached her, its color went from white to gray, and its size from small to large. When it was almost upon her, Chantel saw that the bird's red eyes were full of hatred. Chantel stumbled, fell off the tower and tumbled through the air. Just as she hit the ground, Chantel awoke, covered in a cold sweat.

"What's wrong?" Etam cried as he ran into the tent. "You screamed."

"A nightmare, Etam. Just another nightmare," Chantel answered. Her braid felt very heavy as the cold sweat trickled down her neck. "My guardian is a great gray owl, not a small white owl, but I keep wondering if he's connected in some way to the Spirit of the West or the Wise One of the West."

"I don't know," replied Etam. "But don't worry about that now. Try to get some sleep."

Chantel, however, couldn't stop worrying. Her braid tugged at her scalp, even though she was lying down.

"Something's wrong," Etam said.

"You feel it, too?" asked Chantel. She heard a faint noise, like steam hissing from a boiling kettle, combined with the ringing of cattle chains. "Did you hear that?" she cried, jumping to her feet.

"It's the Evil One! She's found us!" yelled Etam, jumping up. "Run!"

Chantel grabbed her Staff and cloak, and Etam pushed her out of the tent. She stumbled backwards. There was an earsplitting **CRACK!**

A lightning bolt zigzagged through the air, hitting the tent, tearing it in two and engulfing it in red light. It threw Chantel high into the air, and she landed hard in the sand far away.

"ETAM!" she cried. "ETAM!"

There was no response.

"ETAM!" she cried again.

The tent was completely gone. All that was left was a pile of scorched blackened sand.

CHAPTER TWENTY-FIVE

Witnesses

Aquila Bellum, running with the Sand Divers close behind him, saw the red light and heard the explosion. Before he had a chance to think about what it meant, the Evil One's voice filled his mind.

"She is approaching from the south. Be ready to capture her."

"Capture her?" he thought. "I'll do better than that. I will kill her."

"No, Aquila. We need her to get all the relics."

"Yes, the other relics. I will torture her and she will tell us where they are!" Aquila laughed hysterically.

Aquila ordered his Sand Divers to dig a deep hole and fill it with loose sand, creating a pit of quicksand. Then he ordered them to hide. As he watched them bury into the sand, he sensed that Chantel was very near.

"Why can I sense her?" he thought. "I only telepathically communicate with evil ones. Chantel is not an evil one. Perhaps it's because she touched the dark power when she released the red lightning bolt." He smiled devilishly. "Or maybe it is her hand on my chest, the scar, that beats like a second heart?" he thought doubtfully.

He hid under his cloak and waited.

⁓·᷍ᵂᵂᵂ⁓

Mouse, Eno and Ilsole were up early that morning and saw a red flash in the desert flying towards the south.

BOOM!

"Oh no!" cried Ilsole. "It's a red lightning bolt!" He began to shake uncontrollably.

"The Evil One must have found Chantel," shouted Mouse, transforming instantly into the Mighty Warrior. "I should have gone with her! I have to go to her at once!"

"You can jump off the mountain. I'll get the Storm Riders to catch you," Eno said. She put her fingers together to form a *V* and brought them to her lips. She took a deep breath and blew through the *V*. A loud shrill whistle split the air. She repeated it several times until she heard a responding whistle coming from the desert on the south side of the mountain.

"Run and jump," she yelled. "They're ready for you."

The Mighty Warrior backed up, gritted his teeth and took a running leap. He soared through the air. The sandstorm below rose up to meet him. Strong arms caught him. He shut his eyes to shield them from the whirling sand.

The Storm Riders quickly surfed down the ridge of the sandstorm on their discs and landed hard on the desert below the mountain. The Mighty Warrior jumped down and began running as fast as he could towards the explosion.

"I'm coming, Chantel!" he yelled.

~~~

Fin was in the mountains when he started to tremble. He turned, looked South and couldn't believe what he saw on the horizon: a red lightning bolt raced along the sky, traveling from west to south.

Despite the pain in his legs and shoulders, Fin quickened his pace. He had to reach the Mountain People—his people— and ask them to help.

"I must convince my people to help Chantel and fight Owl."

~~~

Chantel couldn't stop shaking. She felt empty and hollow like the reed flute that hung around her neck. She mentally sent out messages to Etam, but no matter how hard she concentrated, she got no reply. "He's dead," she thought. "My Soul Mate is dead." She shouted to the winds, "Evil One, I hate you!"

Then she heard the voice in her head. "Yes! Hate me, Princess!"

~~~

Meanwhile, far away, Etam opened his eyes. He'd used his ability to place-shift just before the red lightning bolt hit, but the force of the dark power had sent him to a place he had never been before. He could no longer feel Chantel, and the pain he felt was so intense that he dropped to his knees. After a long time he got up and looked around. He was still in the desert but in a remote area in the far south, where few creatures ventured. He realized that he was in the region of the desert where the Lost Ones wandered, the ones who had fought their dark side and lost their way. The warm wind, filled with their screams and moaning, made shivers run down his spine.

The Evil One's voice disappeared from Chantel's mind as quickly as it had appeared.

Chantel got up. "I must leave this place at once. The Evil One might unleash another lightning bolt. I must return to Storm Mountain and recover the Enchanted Medallion. I must complete this quest."

She began to run. Etam's flute thumped against her chest and whistled softly as the wind blew over it. But it gave her no comfort. She still felt empty inside. Her Soul Mate was gone. Tears flowed down her cheeks. Although she felt like giving up, she forced herself forward. "I won't let the Evil One win!"

Chantel wiped away the tears in her eyes and saw the hazy shape of Storm Mountain in the distance. She started to run again. She ran as fast as she could, keeping her eyes fixed on the mountain ahead. She did not see the change in the sand pattern in front of her. As she fell, she realized, "Sand Divers!"

The sun overhead burned mercilessly. There was no water and no shade. Etam tried to place-shift but he couldn't. He was too weak and still in shock after losing Chantel. He sat down and covered his head the best he could with his ripped shirt. "Soon night will come," he thought. "Before then I must figure out a way to leave this place."

The sand swallowed Chantel like a hungry snake. She struggled against it, trying to climb the sides of the pit, but the harder she tried, the faster she sunk. She felt a hand grasp her ankle and pull her deeper into the sand. Panic filled her. She tried to kick off the hand that tugged on her ankle, but it held tight.

The sand was above her shoulders now, consuming her neck and chin. She sunk deeper and deeper. The sand touched her lips. She closed her mouth. Nobody was there to help her.

Just before the sand covered her eyes, Chantel saw a shadow appear, and she looked into the Snow Walker's eyes. With her last strength she lifted one arm out and reached above her as her head sunk beneath the sand.

Aquila looked at Chantel's thin arm, and the time he saved his sister from the cold waters of the melting glacier flashed through his mind. Without hesitation he grabbed Chantel's hand and carefully pulled with all his might. Chantel's head slowly emerged, and then her shoulders followed. Aquila felt that something or someone was trying to pull her back under. He pulled harder and worried that he might pull her arm out of its socket. As Chantel's hand started to slip out of his, he gave a jerk in desperation. Chantel's ankle broke free from the Sand Diver's grasp. Aquila Bellum fell backwards. Chantel popped out of the sand hole and fell beside him, coughing and sputtering.

After recovering her breath, she turned over and looked into his eyes. They weren't red like she'd remembered. They were crystal blue like hers.

"You saved my life," croaked Chantel. "Why?"

Aquila didn't answer. At that moment, nine Sand Divers emerged out of the sand.

"You saved the enemy! Why?" one of them screamed in disgust.

"Run, Chantel. Run before I change my mind," Aquila whispered as the color of his eyes started to change from crystal blue to red.

Chantel struggled to her feet and took off.

"Get her!" shouted the Sand Divers, taking up pursuit.

She slipped and stumbled. The Sand Divers gained ground. Just as they were about to overpower her, she saw a most wonderful thing: the Mighty Warrior running to her rescue.

With his great sword he sliced through three surprised Sand Divers. Motivated by hatred, the Mighty Warrior fought harder than he ever had before. Chantel had never seen her friend so angry. He turned around, raised his sword over his head and sliced it into the bodies of four more Sand Divers. He turned around again. The remaining two Sand Divers, realizing the fate that awaited them if they attacked, dove into the sand to escape. The Mighty Warrior jumped forward and stabbed his sword up to its hilt into the sand twice in quick succession. The sand turned red.

All the Sand Divers were dead. Victorious, the Mighty Warrior turned to Chantel.

"How did you find me?" she asked.

"I headed towards the place where the red lightning bolt struck. I knew that you were in danger the moment I saw it," he replied. "I should have accompanied you in the first place. I'm supposed to be your protector, aren't I?"

"You are! Thank you, my friend," said Chantel. "You arrived just in time. But where is Aquila Bellum?" she added, scanning the surrounding sea of sand. "Did you see him?"

"The Snow Walker!" exclaimed the Mighty Warrior. "What's he doing way out here? I only saw nine Sand Divers. We'd better not wait around and give that monster a chance to attack."

As the Mighty Warrior began the journey back to Storm Mountain, carrying Chantel on his back, Chantel's mind churned over. "Aquila, a monster? But he just saved me. Why would he do that?"

From his hiding place under his cloak, Aquila Bellum watched as the Mighty Warrior and Chantel disappeared into the distance. Aquila was still in shock; he'd saved the Princess of Freedom and let her escape, and there were no living witnesses to report what he had done. The Mighty Warrior had taken care of that.

He shook the sand out of his cloak and put it back on. Then he sat on a dune and cradled his head in his hands. "What's wrong with me?" he moaned. "Why did Chantel remind me of Procella? Why do I keep thinking about my family? I am not part of that family anymore. They no longer exist. I made sure of that myself.

"Does the Evil One know what I have just done? If she does, the only way to make her trust me again would be to kill Chantel once and for all, but the Evil One told me that I should not kill Chantel because she is the only one who could get me the Golden Sword. But I know how to take care of that. Before killing her, I'll force her to tell me how to get the Sword and the other relics. And if she refuses! Ha! I'll torture her until she reveals that knowledge!"

When he rose, his eyes were red and full of hatred again.

"All is not yet lost," Aquila Bellum thought. "I will return to Enim Ymene and his Sand Divers. Chantel and her friend are returning to Storm Mountain, but they will come down from there once again. And when they do, I will be ready with an army. Chantel is still mine, and soon her Golden Braid will decorate my fireplace, right beside the mountain goat's head."

CHAPTER TWENTY-SIX

Alive

When Chantel and Mouse finally made it back to the top of Storm Mountain, they were exhausted. Eno, Tac, Ilsole and Fox were all greatly relieved to see them alive.

"Are you hurt?" asked Eno.

"Yes," Chantel said, her voice cracking. "The red lightning bolt killed Etam." Chantel's shoulders drooped, and she stared at the ground. Her face was covered with dust, except for the lines on her cheeks where tears had washed it away.

"Are you sure he is dead?" asked Eno. "Etam is a swift place-shifter."

"I saw the destroyed tent with my own eyes," replied Chantel.

"Let's find out for certain," Eno said.

Chantel raised her eyebrows and looked at Eno with sad, tired eyes.

"Since you reawakened my Inner Light, all my talents have come back," explained Eno. "Sit beside me and watch."

Facing south, Eno sat cross-legged on the ground and

closed her eyes. The sand in front of her started to vibrate slowly—first just a little and then in small peaked waves—until it began to transform into various shapes. One shape was a small tent, and two other shapes looked like humans. Then the tent flattened, and the two humans were thrown in opposite directions.

"The Evil One took Etam away," intoned Eno. "She tried to kill him, but he place-shifted before she could. He is still alive, but the lightning bolt severed the bond that connects you. You can no longer communicate with him through visions or mind speech. That's why you feel so empty."

The sand in front of Eno shifted again. It formed a mountain on which one human sat, and far away the other human shape stood in a flat area.

"There he is, at the end of the desert. He is in the land of the Lost Ones. I hope he will stay sane. The screams and moaning of those who have transformed can drive one mad."

The sand flattened out and did not move again.

"But . . . but the red lightning bolt," Chantel stammered. "I saw it strike."

"Etam first made sure that you were safe; then he vanished. Mother Nature taught him how to move very quickly. But don't worry. One day you will surely see him again. It is said that when the Evil One is defeated, all Soul Mates will reconnect with each other. Etam is strong. He will find his way back. And if he can't make it by himself, the Spirit of the South will help him."

She stopped abruptly, refocused and reentered the trancelike state for a few moments and said, "In fact, she's helping him right now. She has sent two Desert Runners to guide him back to safety."

"Thank you, Eno," said Chantel. She touched the reed flute hanging from her neck. "There is only one thing left to do here," she thought, "and I will do it tonight."

CHAPTER TWENTY-SEVEN

The Enchanted Medallion

After dinner, after the others had gone to sleep, Chantel joined Eno outside. The silvery blue moon and the stars sparkled in the sky.

"I've been finding it difficult to sleep," said Eno. "Since you lit my Inner Light, I've had so much energy. There is so much I want to do. The first thing I must do, however, is show you . . ."

"The path to the Enchanted Medallion," said Chantel, completing Eno's sentence. "I'm ready."

"So you have the Key?"

Chantel showed her the golden flute. "Etam said that this will guide me to the Enchanted Medallion."

"And so it will. Follow me."

Eno led the way down the stairs to the bottom of Storm Mountain. This time Chantel clung close to the wall, but she looked down and saw the exquisite beauty of the labyrinth inside Storm Mountain. The bright rays of the moon shone through the cracks of the mountain and reflected off the walls, casting silvery beams of light throughout the labyrinth. Chantel saw the many colored flowers that grew along the numerous paths that twisted and turned like rivers. She listened to the musical sounds of the wind that made its way through the many canyons and crevasses. Small trees and bushes climbed up the cliffs. Others grew out of the side of the mountain walls while still others graced the labyrinth's paths. Their leaves draped the labyrinth in countless shades of green.

They reached the bottom and entered the labyrinth. After walking for a few minutes, Eno pointed to the beginning of one particular path. It was narrower than the ones they had walked so far. Yellow flowers grew along the walls, forming an archway across the entrance.

"It's through there," said Eno. "Only you can retrieve the Medallion from its Keeper. I don't know how, but the flute will help you succeed. I will wait for you here."

"Thank you, Eno. I will see you soon."

Chantel walked alone into the labyrinth. Ivy curled up the sides of the path. The air was cool and refreshing.

Soon she came to a junction. The path split off in three directions. Blue flowers surrounded one opening, red flowers another, and yellow flowers the third.

"Which one to take?" thought Chantel.

She pointed the flute at the paths, but that did nothing. She put it to her lips. When she blew into it, it sounded awful, like the groaning of an old tree bending in a storm. She concentrated, trying to remember the evening she'd played the flute for the sand creatures and Etam Luos. She blew a little bit stronger and covered three holes in the flute with her fingers, and this time a clear note piped forth. She lifted up one finger and then another in the pattern Etam had taught her. Although the simple tune sounded much better, nothing happened to show her which way to go. There was no light, no beckoning creature, and no signal of any sort. Chantel's hopes dropped and she stopped playing.

Then she heard a faint song coming from the path to the right, the one surrounded by blue flowers. It was an echo of her tune, like a bird responding to another bird's call in the woods. She quickly headed down that path. When she came to another juncture, she played the flute again. Again a musical echo directed her choice. She walked and played, following the sounds she heard, which became clearer and louder as she continued deeper into the labyrinth.

Finally, after turning a corner, she came upon a large open space. In the center stood a giant leafless tree. As she approached it, she noticed that instead of leaves, hundreds of medallions hung from the tree's drooping branches.

The medallions were made of different metals studded with priceless jewels. No doubt their weight caused the branches to droop so much. As Chantel played the flute, she listened to the tune's echo and watched the tree shake its branches, which made the medallions swing back and forth, hitting each other. It sounded like a giant wind chime. She tried to locate the source of the echo, but it seemed to be coming from the tree. She stopped playing.

"Which is the right one?" Chantel wondered. "I saw this place through Eno's eyes, but I can't remember."

There were golden medallions, copper ones and silver ones. Many had rubies, diamonds and emeralds mounted on them. Chantel would have taken them all if she could have; they were so beautiful. She was mystified as to which one to choose. A voice piped up in her mind. "Take the large one, the one with the gold star and the diamond in the middle. It is the loveliest. It is a medallion meant for a princess."

Chantel moved closer to the tree. "Yes," she said. "The big golden medallion. It sparkles as brightly as the Golden Sword. That must be it."

The golden shine of the medallion flickered in her eyes, and Chantel slowly moved forward as if in a daze, tempted by her greed. She reached out to touch it, and as she did, the ground beneath her feet trembled. A small crack in the ground behind her opened up. As it grew larger, smaller cracks branched out from it and moved towards Chantel's feet. As Chantel's hand moved closer to the golden medallion, the cracks widened. Chantel, mesmerized by the dazzling medallion, did not realize what was happening around her, her mind clouded by the Darkness that tempted her.

CHAPTER TWENTY-EIGHT

Haunted by the Past

The Wise Ones are not much different than other living beings. They also experience pain and the fear of losing loved ones. What sets them apart is their strength to overcome these pains and hardships and refocus quickly. What may leave us in the misery of self-doubt, anguish and dismay only strengthens a Wise One. But watch out; after the Evil One awakes, the Wise Ones are in danger of becoming like us—full of fear and weakness, unable to stand up for the ones they have to protect.

From The Book of Erebus

Eno sat on a rock surrounded by blue flowers and watched Chantel disappear into the labyrinth. She was confident that Chantel would find the Medallion. She closed her eyes, remembering why she had hidden it there. With her Inner Light burning brightly, Eno was not afraid to let herself remember now.

Eight moon crossings ago, she attended a meeting in the castle in the center of the four lands. There they discussed the destruction of the Winged Ones. Upon her return home, the Sand Divers were waiting for them. What happened after that was a horrible memory she had constantly fought to repress.

"Chantel is only twelve years old and is carrying a heavy burden for us all," she thought. "She needs and deserves all the help we can give."

At that moment, Eno swore an oath that she would try to reunite the desert tribes and help Chantel succeed in her quest.

Eno opened her eyes, pulled into the present by the faint music of the reed flute. It reminded her of the music of the horse breeders, and the faces of her three close friends who had died such horrible deaths appeared in front of her.

She sighed and whispered, "Farewell, my good friends. May you live happily in the afterworld. I will never forget you."

Enim had a restless night, his sleep haunted by nightmares about the Wise One of the South. "What can I do to end this torment?" he thought, waking up in a sweat. "What can I do to make amends?"

"Get the Enchanted Medallion and kill the Wise One," an angry voice replied.

He jumped up with a yell and faced Aquila Bellum, who was standing inside his tent.

"Aquila! What are you doing here? What happened? Did you kill Chantel?" Enim asked. "Where are my Sand Divers?"

Aquila towered over him. Although he looked tired and was covered with sand, his red eyes sparked brighter than ever.

"She is not dead, but your Sand Divers are, as you will be if you don't pull yourself together. Don't think the Evil One can't hear your thoughts! I heard your questionings loud and clear in my mind. We have to get ready to intercept Chantel. The sun is rising in the East. Get your Sand Divers into position. She will eventually come this way."

Enim followed Aquila out of the tent. Aquila's wolverine, lying in the sand nearby, growled and bounded over to Aquila.

As Enim yelled commands to his Sand Divers, Aquila hunched beside his wolverine. As the wolverine licked Aquila's hand with his blue tongue, Aquila muttered, "We have to get ready. I think this is my last chance."

CHAPTER TWENTY-NINE

Simplicity

Chantel reached for the golden medallion. As her hand got closer and closer, her Golden Braid grew heavier and heavier until it felt like it was weighted down by metal medallions itself. She pulled back her hand, and her braid grew a little lighter. Chantel understood. She pulled back her hand completely and stepped away from the tree. The cracks in the ground stopped growing, too.

Obviously the big golden medallion with the diamond was not the right one.

"The Enchanted Medallion must represent desert values: simplicity," thought Chantel. "Simplicity." As she repeated the word, she stared at the tree, searching once again. She looked at each medallion, and then she saw it.

She instantly knew that it was the right one, for it was more beautiful than all the others put together.

The Enchanted Medallion was a wooden ring the size of Chantel's palm that hung from a leather thong on a branch on the backside of the tree. In its center was a single green stone held in place by black leather thongs crisscrossing the wooden ring. Chantel removed the Medallion from the branch and held it in her hand. The green stone began to glow, and the tree came alive and began to twist.

"You have chosen well, Princess of Freedom," the tree said in a deep, loud voice. It shook its branches, and all the medallions clanked against each other again.

"You have learned much about yourself and about our values. It is important to know thyself, because it is you yourself you must ultimately rely on. Remember: simplicity and loyalty. Well done. You must go now. They are waiting for you."

The ground shook.

"Who's waiting for me?" Chantel asked, hanging the Medallion around her neck. It was light and felt warm.

"Friends and enemies," the tree responded. "Watch out for the unexpected and listen to your inner voice. You still have a long way to go before you are ready. My time here is done. I am ready to meet my friends below. But your time is just beginning. Now, go! Quickly!"

The ground shook again, and cracks grew from the ground around the tree's trunk. Chantel turned around and ran as fast as she could, following the blue flowers that grew along the path. Behind her the earth opened up like a great mouth, and the tree, along with all the glittering medallions dangling from its limbs, vanished into the earth.

A yellow light appeared above the large hole. A voice filled the space. "You protected our relic well, ancient one, Keeper of the labyrinth. I will see you again soon."

The tree's voice rose from the hole in reply. "Yes, Spirit of the South. Next time it will be in your world."

The earth closed again and only a flat empty space remained.

~~~

Chantel heard the loud growling and crashing behind her, but she didn't dare look back. When Chantel reached the labyrinth entrance, Eno gave a great sigh of relief. "I was worried. The whole earth shook! Come. Our friends will be worried about us."

Eno and Chantel reached the top of the mountain just as the sun reached its highest position in the bright blue sky. Mouse, who had transformed into the Mighty Warrior, was pacing in front of the tent. Ilsole and Fox were anxiously flying in circles above.

"I've got it!" cried Chantel, showing them the wooden medallion hanging around her neck beside the golden flute.

Hardly giving the Medallion a glance, Mouse hurriedly said, "Look to the North! See that cloud of dust on the horizon?"

Eno and Chantel went over to the northern side of Storm Mountain and saw what Mouse was pointing at.

"The Warlord and his evil ones are gathering," Mouse continued. "I've been watching them since you left this morning. They're blocking our way back to the North."

"They are waiting for you, Chantel," said Eno.

"Yes. They are going to try to stop me from returning home."

"But they won't succeed," said Mouse. "I will be with you."

"And so will I," said Eno.

Chantel turned and went into the tent to gather her belongings. When she came out, the Mighty Warrior, Fox, Tac, Ilsole and Eno Esiw were ready to go. Chantel stared at Eno. She was wearing the protective gear of a Storm Rider.

"Yes, Chantel, my tribe is the tribe of the Storm Riders," Eno said.

"Let's go and meet the enemy!" Chantel said confidently, even though she was nervous and frightened. She did not want to confront Aquila Bellum. He had rescued her, but she knew he had changed back to his dark side and was her enemy again.

Eno whistled through her fingers several times. Hearing a whistle in return, they all ran to the northern side of the mountaintop and jumped off the edge. The protective storms rose to meet them with the Storm Riders ready to pick each one of them up, except for Eno and Chantel. Eno floated through the air and raced down the sandstorm on her own disk with Chantel standing beside her.

CHAPTER THIRTY

Back in the Mountains

Fin looked down from the top of the mountain range. He could just make out the Lake of Clouds in the distance. His heart filled with joy and happiness. He couldn't wait to see Aurora again.

"I wonder if she's changed," he thought. "How long has it been? At least seven moon crossings."

As he looked around he realized how much had changed. The mountain slopes used to be covered with green pine trees. Now most of them had lost their needles and looked like sad skeletons. Only a few bushes still grew along the lake's shore. The area was covered with snow, and Fin remembered the summers when the whole area had been grassy and lush. Now, even with all the snow around, everything looked gray and dead. It was the Evil One's doing, a sign of the spreading Darkness.

Fin was focused so intently on the downward path that he didn't notice the movement behind a couple of dead trees on the side of the slope, nor did he notice the absence of mountain birds and their lovely songs.

By the time Fin did notice that something was wrong, it was too late. The wolverines and hyenas attacked. One wolverine jumped on Fin's back. A strong paw with sharp claws cut through his cloak and into his skin. Fin felt a sharp pain and warm blood running down his back. He fell forward and tumbled down the steep slope. The wolverines and hyenas chased after him, growling madly. They could smell Fin's blood. Fin landed hard on his back at the bottom of the slope. He tried to get up, but he knew it was no use. There were too many of them. He was defenseless. The beasts approached slowly. There were eight of them—four wolverines and four hyenas. They growled and gnashed their teeth. As they got closer, their approach slowed. They sniffed, enjoying the smell of fear that came from Fin.

Fin's mind raced. He saw Chantel's face in front of him, smiling. The fact that he would never see her again made him sad. He would never know if she completed her quest. His back hurt badly, and tears ran down his cheeks. He hadn't thought that his life would end this way.

A quiet hissing sound penetrated the deadly calm. One of the hyenas howled in pain, arched in the air and landed on his back. A long arrow stuck out of its chest, and the snow underneath the fallen beast turned red. Ten more arrows hissed down the slope. Horrible howls filled the air as arrows struck the beasts. Finally all was silent. The beasts lay dead.

Fin tried to get up, but he was too weak from the loss of blood. His ears rang from the hyenas' howls. He propped himself to a sitting position and looked around. Humanlike shapes dressed in white seemed to be floating towards him.

"Spirits?" he figured. But the ghostly shapes weren't spirits at all; they were Mountain People.

"Eronimus Finsh?" a woman asked. "Of all the people in the world, you are the last one I expected to see. What are you doing here?"

"I came here to see Aurora," Fin said weakly, and with that, he slipped into unconsciousness.

"Take him to the City of Ice," Aurora said to her companions. "I have to examine his wound."

Four strong men lifted Fin up. "Be careful and gentle," Aurora said. "This man is very important to us."

With Aurora leading the way, the men brought Fin to the Lake of Clouds. They did not stop when they reached the lake's misty shores but continued on down the slope, disappearing into the waves of clouds.

They had failed to notice that one of the wolverines was only injured and not dead. That wounded wolverine observed how the Mountain People vanished into the lake without getting wet, and he realized that he had just discovered his enemies' hiding place. After all the Mountain People had vanished, he growled weakly and got up slowly.

With his strong teeth, he broke off the end of the arrow stuck in his left shoulder. Then he turned and limped up the slope to Aquila's cave, eager to report to his master.

CHAPTER THIRTY-ONE

Another Fight

One of the Sand Divers came running towards Aquila and Enim, who were sitting on the ground, plotting how to kill Chantel.

"Look!" he yelled as he reached the two warlords. "Storm Mountain is burning."

Aquila jumped up quickly and turned to face south.

"That is not a fire, you idiot," he hissed aggressively. "It is a cloud of dust. I wonder what happened."

Enim rolled over in the sand, got onto his knees and stood up with difficulty. Aquila watched him and shook his head in disgust.

"If you get any fatter, your Sand Divers could roll you around like a ball. You would probably get around faster that way," he growled. "Do you know what those storm clouds mean?"

"Yes, I think so," Enim said, ignoring Aquila's insult.

"So what do they mean? Tell me."

"I think it tells us that Chantel has found the Enchanted

Medallion and is leaving Storm Mountain. I've been right all these years: it was hidden inside the mountain all along. I don't know exactly where the clouds of dust are headed, but I think we should get ready."

"I am ready. You just have to get your Sand Divers ready. I will organize all the others who have joined us. Let's surprise Chantel and her friends. She probably expects only you, the Sand Divers and me. I can't wait to face her again."

Enim turned around and walked towards his army of Sand Divers.

"Remember," Aquila yelled after him. "This time we kill her."

The Storm Riders landed smoothly, and Chantel and her friends stepped off the sand gliders. She had almost come to enjoy the wild rides in the sandstorm.

"Will the Storm Riders join us?" Chantel asked.

"Yes," answered Eno.

"So what do we do now?" the Mighty Warrior asked as he had pulled out his long sword and looked down at Chantel. She looked up at him and smiled.

"Another battle, but this time we are not alone," she said.

"Yes," the Mighty Warrior said. "I almost feel sorry for the evil ones."

He smiled back at Chantel, who besides having her Magic Staff in one hand now had her sword in the other.

"Why don't you just turn invisible?" Fox asked as he landed on Chantel's shoulder.

"I would, but I can't hold on to that power long enough." Chantel turned to the Mighty Warrior, who was looking out across the sand. "How many of them do you think there are?" she asked.

"I see several brown hyenas, one wolverine, many warthogs, a few wild dogs, plenty of Sand Divers and many small creepy crawlers—about forty of them in total—plus Aquila Bellum and Enim Ymene," the Mighty Warrior reported.

Chantel could see Aquila in the distance. Her new sense of being able to see through others' eyes began to tempt her once again.

"What is Aquila thinking?" she wondered. "Why are we connected?"

"You could find out," said a voice inside, tempting her.

"No. I must not. The Growers of the West warned me not to use this power. It will only bring trouble, like it did with Eno," Chantel argued with herself.

"But in the end I did help Eno. She was upset, but it spurred the meditation and the trip to the Growers. My looking into her memories saved her. Perhaps I could save Aquila. Or Enim. I could try the new power on him. His mind will tell me what they are planning. Maybe he has set a trap. Mouse or Eno might get killed. I could save them," Chantel reasoned with herself.

"You don't need to," another voice in her head asserted. "Remember what the Growers said and what Eno said: it's wrong to invade others' minds. It is the Evil One's power."

"Do it, Chantel. Save your friends," the other voice yelled encouragingly. "You can save your friends or lose them to the afterworld. Save them!"

"No, Chantel! Don't!"

It was too late. The orange light was already flickering in the Magic Staff's crystal. Chantel had already begun to concentrate and to seek out Enim, the Warlord of the South. She looked into endless tubes and suddenly heard his voice in one. She followed it and saw Aquila Bellum. He looked at her and his eyes narrowed.

"Are you all right, Enim?" he asked. "Your eyes have changed."

"Someone's in my mind, and it isn't the Evil One!" cried Enim. "I feel you, Princess of Freedom!"

Chantel panicked and suddenly she couldn't breathe. She felt as though a cold hand had grabbed her throat.

"Gotcha!" the Evil One said. "Now let me see what I can do with you."

Chantel tried to breathe but couldn't. The drowning feeling returned.

The blood pulsated in Chantel's veins, and she heard the Evil One say, "You are weak. You followed your temptation. That is good, because now I know that you and I are very much alike. The Darkness is getting closer, and one day you will understand me. I need you. So fight well, my princess. You have to live so that we can meet."

Chantel dropped to her knees.

"Now I can see you, Princess," the Evil One continued. "You are pretty, and the Golden Braid suits you well."

"Chantel!" Eno cried, kneeling beside her. "What's happening?"

"The Evil One," Chantel said. "She now knows what I look like. She's in my mind and in my memories."

Tears filled her eyes.

"But how?" cried Eno.

"I used the gift from the Evil One," Chantel whispered. "The orange light . . . the Darkness . . ."

"Seek your Inner Light, and you will cast off whoever has control of you," cried Eno.

Chantel's body shook, but Eno's touch calmed her. Chantel concentrated on her light. It blazed. The choking feeling subsided. Chantel took a deep breath and rubbed her neck.

"What happened?" asked the Mighty Warrior, kneeling by her other side.

"You warned me, but I didn't listen. I didn't listen. I . . . I tried to use the orange power, on Enim. But he knew I was there; the Darkness tempted me and I fell for it. I am weak," Chantel exclaimed. "And then the Evil One was there . . . "

"No, you're not weak," said Eno, helping Chantel up. "You are strong enough to push the Evil One out of your mind."

The Mighty Warrior looked at Chantel, worried. "We all get tempted and fall at one time or another. You show strength by realizing you've done wrong. And you show strength by standing up again."

CHAPTER THIRTY-TWO

Aurora

When they reached the City of Ice under the Lake of Clouds, Fin woke to the dazzling light of the crystal- and ice-sculpted city. As beautiful as it was, Fin knew that it was merely a glorified prison. Protection from the Evil One and her beasts came at a cost: hidden under the clouds, there was no sun, no stars, and no moons.

The Mountain Men carried Fin into one of the castle's guest rooms and laid him down on his stomach on a large bed covered with white linens. Aurora examined his back and began to clean and bandage his wounds.

"You were lucky, Fin," she said. "The cuts are not deep. But what happened to your shoulders? I can see some older puncture wounds that are infected."

"Those wounds are the reason I was seeking you," Fin replied. "But first, before I explain, thank you for rescuing me."

"I'm telling you again, you were very lucky," Aurora said. "A mountain bird told us that a man was traveling towards our area with wolverines and hyenas on the hunt for him. Thus we knew that we were needed. We usually do not leave the city. It is too dangerous, for there is always a chance that we might give away the location of our hiding spot, but we knew that the man the bird described would surely be killed by those beasts if we did not intervene. So we arrived just in time, and here we are." She stepped back and added, "There. I've finished bandaging your back."

Fin turned around to get a better look at Aurora. Her hair was as white as her cloak, and instead of being braided into three strands, it formed a single strong one. Resting on her forehead was a silver diadem, the sign of the leader of the Mountain People.

"You have changed," Fin said slowly.

"So have you, Eronimus Finsh. We haven't seen each other in a long time," Aurora replied. "So, why did you need to see us? What has finally brought you back to your people?"

"What do you think about Chantel?"

"She is strong and true of heart. I believe she will save us," Aurora said confidently.

"Chantel, the Princess of Freedom, needs your help," said Fin. "She is in great danger without knowing it. I have a terrible suspicion that the one who raised her is an evil one. I think he tried to kill me."

"Owl?" exclaimed Aurora. "Are you sure? The last time I saw him was eight moon crossings ago, when we retrieved the Golden Sword. At that time he had sworn an oath to Mother Nature to protect Chantel with his life."

"I don't know about that. I believe he tried to kill me," replied Fin. "I don't remember exactly what happened, but

I was staying with him in the castle, and then I was lying on a ledge in the Endless Gorge, half-dead. The Rock Climber who rescued me gave me this. I was holding it in my hand when I fell." Fin pulled out the feather from his pocket.

"A gray feather?"

"Yes. I'm sure it's one of Owl's feathers," Fin explained. "If I only could contact Mother Nature . . . but Chantel has blocked the doors to my mind and thus to my talents."

For the first time, Aurora looked at Fin suspiciously. "And why did she do that?"

"If Chantel returns to her castle and Owl is an evil one," continued Fin, ignoring the question, "who knows what might happen to her? You have to help her. Will you send some of your soldiers to the castle to protect Chantel?"

"Because of a single feather? This is a serious allegation, Fin. Owl has raised Chantel since she was a baby. What would change his nature?" asked Aurora. Then she added, "I will need time to decide. I must meet with the council."

As Aurora left the room, questions filled her thoughts. "Why would Chantel close the doors to your mind, Fin?" she wondered. "Did she lose trust in you? And if so, why? What did you do? And why should I trust you now?"

CHAPTER THIRTY-THREE

The Sand Divers' Trap

Ilsole and Fox flew in the sky and watched Chantel, Eno, Tac and the Mighty Warrior march towards their enemies. The Storm Riders spread out and followed them.

Chantel had to recover fast; she concentrated on how to use the powers of the Magic Staff properly. Eno had taught her well. She meditated while they were walking and called upon the power. Slowly and gradually it grew in Chantel.

They were getting closer to their enemies, and Chantel could see their angry faces. Aquila Bellum was standing among them, looking straight at her with his red eyes.

The army of Sand Divers and evil ones was ready. They stood in a v-shape formation.

As Chantel and her friends approached, the Sand Divers began to stomp their feet. A monotone rhythm pulsated throughout the otherwise quiet desert. Chantel stopped. She was tense, holding her Magic Staff and her sword with sweaty hands. The Mighty Warrior stood calm and focused beside her. Eno and Tac stood on Chantel's other side. Their eyes were fixed on Enim Ymene.

The Sand Divers yelled and screamed and ran towards the four friends. The Mighty Warrior got into position.

The warthogs reached them first. They charged with their heads down and their razor-sharp teeth pointed forward. Chantel pointed her Staff at them and, thinking of the color blue and wind, she created a small tornado that picked them up and shook them around. Chantel stopped the tornado before it grew too large, and when the tornado dissipated, the warthogs banged into each other and landed unconscious on the ground.

"Hyenas at your back!" cried Fox from above.

Chantel spun around and called upon the powers of wind again. The winds built up, and walls of sand crumbled onto the hyenas, muffling their yelps and eventually burying them completely. An army of scorpions scuttled over the newly built sand bank, but Chantel quickly created fires that made the small creatures scurry away and look for cover. The colors in the crystal at the end of her Magic Staff changed from yellow to green to indigo to blue.

While Chantel fought one group of creatures after another, Eno, her Storm Riders and the Mighty Warrior attacked the Sand Divers and wild dogs. The Mighty Warrior's sword flew through the air, slicing Sand Divers in two. With his other paw, he smashed them down into the sand. Eno protected the Mighty Warrior from a pack of wild dogs that tried to jump onto his shoulders to bury their teeth into his neck.

Ilsole and Fox flew up and down, picking up desert rats and sandworms, lifting them up high into the air and dropping them to their deaths. Ilsole tried to keep up with Fox, who was flying up and down as fast as an attacking eagle, but he was still weak and soon had to rest by just gliding through the air.

Tac zigzagged in front of another pack of wild dogs, leading them on a chase away from the fighting area and into a sinkhole. Before the wild dogs realized what was happening, the sand sucked them under. Tac, very pleased with herself, dashed back into the fray to repeat the maneuver.

Just as it seemed that Chantel and her friends were going to win the battle, something terrible happened.

Chantel didn't notice some strange movements in the sand under her feet.

Enim Ymene had momentarily entered Chantel's mind and body when she had used the orange light to enter his mind, and while he was there he had felt the Enchanted Medallion hanging around her neck. The knowledge exhilarated him, and he instructed two of his Sand Divers to sneak up underneath her, drag her under the sand and snatch it from her.

Four hands came out of the sand and grabbed Chantel by her ankles, pulling her down.

"MOUSE!" she cried.

He spun around and pushed his sword into the ground beside Chantel several times, trying to hit the creatures underneath without hitting Chantel's half-buried body. With one paw, he grabbed her arms just before the ground swallowed her completely and pulled her out.

"Are you okay?"

"I'm fine," said Chantel, gripping her Staff. "Behind you! Watch out!"

The Mighty Warrior kicked out his large hind foot and knocked a warthog unconscious before turning back to Chantel. "We're winning. Soon the fight will be over. Have you seen Enim? Or Aquila?"

Chantel shook her head. As she did so, she could feel that something was different. There was a different amount of weight hanging from her neck. She looked down.

"The Enchanted Medallion! They stole the Enchanted Medallion!"

While the Mighty Warrior and the Storm Riders shielded her, she dropped to her hands and knees and searched the ground. She couldn't see anything. She sifted and dug through the hot sand, but it wasn't there.

Then she heard a triumphant yell.

"Over here, little Princess!" Enim Ymene voice bellowed across the battlefield.

The fighting froze. Everyone turned towards Enim, who waved the Enchanted Medallion in the air from its leather thong.

"Time for you to give up! I have the medallion! You thought you were so smart when you entered my mind. Ha! I control the desert now!"

"NO!" cried Chantel.

"You don't believe me? Let's start with your big friend."

Enim Ymene held the Enchanted Medallion with both of his hands. The green stone in the middle of the Medallion began to shine like a strange star. A dark green light traveled across the ground until it engulfed the Mighty Warrior.

The Mighty Warrior dropped his sword. Voices, including Enim's, that traveled with the green light filled the Mighty Warrior's mind. He covered his ears with his paws, but it was no use. His mind spun in a confusion of wild thoughts—dark thoughts overwhelming all the others thoughts in his mind.

"Join the Darkness and you will receive riches beyond your dreams," Enim's voice screamed in the Mighty Warrior's head.

The Mighty Warrior's huge, strong body started to shiver, and he changed back to a little orange mouse.

"Join the Darkness!" echoed the other voices. "When you do, you will be rich! You will have lots of food! I will give you gold and diamonds. You can impress your parents by getting them new furniture and a new, larger den. You could impress all your family friends. They will no longer care that you are different. They will forget that you once destroyed their house. They will all love you. Join the Darkness. Join me, and you will find perfect happiness."

Mouse rocked his head between his tiny paws. He moaned.

"Don't be confused," crackled the dark thoughts. "It is all so simple. Join the Darkness and you will be happy and loved."

Mouse, however, did not give in. He battled the dark thoughts with more strength than Enim had expected. Enim didn't realize that Mouse had experience in fighting dark thoughts when he was younger. He was not going to give in easily.

Enim didn't want to waste any more time with Mouse. He moved the Enchanted Medallion up and down. The green light began to force Mouse into the sand against his will.

Chantel watched in pain as her friend sunk deeper and deeper. There was only one thing she could do. The color in the crystal at the end of her Magic Staff changed to blue, and she became invisible. Nobody seemed to notice; they were all so focused on Mouse's plight. She crept towards Enim, undetectable except for a trail of small footprints in the soft sand.

"Kill him!" Enim yelled to his Sand Divers. Two Sand Divers jumped on the little mouse and dragged him below the sand while Enim laughed hysterically. He turned to face Chantel, but she was gone.

Aquila, who had been watching everything nearby, leapt in front of Enim, breaking the thread of green light. Aquila's eyes were fastened on the trail of small footprints leading to the pot-bellied warlord. Aquila pushed his hand forward again and again into what seemed to be thin air.

"What are you doing?" yelled Enim.

Aquila's hand finally struck Chantel in the chest. She fell down. When she hit the ground, she lost the connection to the blue power and became visible once again. She lay in front of Aquila and Enim. Her Staff had fallen out of her hand, and Aquila stood on it with one foot. Without her Staff, she couldn't call on her powers. She was helpless.

Enim was about to direct the light of the Enchanted Medallion at Chantel when Eno leaped between them.

"Stop!" she cried. "You have done enough harm!" Her eyes blazed furiously. "You have to kill me before you kill the Princess of Freedom!"

"Do it!" Aquila yelled at Enim. "Use the power of the Enchanted Medallion to kill the Wise One of the South."

Enim, remembering his awful dreams, hesitated. The terrible things he had done to Eno became visible in his mind again. His hand began to tremble. The green light became stronger, but Enim was not able to direct it at Eno. The light radiated from the stone and become brighter and more intense as it slowly surrounded Enim. The Medallion shook in his hand. His face changed; it was no longer angry and hateful but sad and ashamed. He lowered his eyes away from Eno's eyes. Memories of his evil side came rushing into his head.

"Those screams have to stop," he thought. He knew that he couldn't hurt his Wise One again. He looked back into her blue eyes and smiled.

"Could you ever forgive me, Eno?" he whispered so that only she could hear it.

He felt the power of the Enchanted Medallion grow stronger and stronger, and he knew that if he did not release it, it would kill him. His head turned back and he looked up into the blue sky. He heard Aquila yell at him through a heavy fog, but the memories of what he had done to Eno screamed louder. Enim made his choice and held on to the Enchanted Medallion.

"Drop the Medallion, Enim!" Eno yelled. "The power in it is growing. If you don't release it you will die."

"Use the power to kill her!" bellowed Aquila.

But Enim didn't want to kill Eno, nor did he want to give up the object he'd desired for so long.

The dark green light blazing from the stone of the Medallion grew brighter still. Enim's hand began to burn.

His body started to shrivel as if all his life force was being sucked right out of him. The dark green light returned into the stone, and Enim fell to the ground. A strong shock wave traveled through the air, leveling everything and everyone standing around him. The Enchanted Medallion flew through the air.

Slowly the dust and sand settled. In the middle of a scorched ring of sand lay Enim's body. He looked like a dried flower, his skin gray and shriveled, his limbs twisted and deformed, his head small. Enim was dead.

CHAPTER THIRTY-FOUR

Covered with Sand

Eno lay beside Chantel. Both were covered in thin blankets of sand. Ilsole and Fox landed beside them as they groaned and sat up. Tac paced the area where Mouse had been buried. "Oh, Mouse, where are you?" she meowed.

The ground started to vibrate, and with a sudden explosion the Mighty Warrior rose out of the sand to everyone's great relief. The few Sand Divers who hadn't been killed or thrown away by the blast dove into the sand and disappeared.

"Where is Aquila Bellum?" asked the Mighty Warrior, scanning the battle area. "Is he dead?"

"I don't think so. He escaped again," said Chantel. "But don't worry, Mouse. It's okay. I'm glad he did."

Mouse looked at her, puzzled. "Your most dangerous enemy escapes, and you're glad?"

"I'll explain later," replied Chantel. "Let's hurry. Soon it will be dark, and we have to find the Enchanted Medallion."

The Medallion was not with Enim, nor was it anywhere near his body. Mouse and Eno looked around. The area around them was covered with dead Sand Divers, wild dogs, warthogs and scorpions.

"It could be anywhere. It could be buried under the sand," Mouse said. "We'll never find it."

"We have to!" said Chantel. "I'm not giving up now! Not after all this!" She stomped her foot in frustration and felt the flute bounce against her chest. The flute! It had found the Medallion the first time; surely it could help her again, she thought.

She pulled it out and started to play Etam Luos' song. The notes filled the air and crossed over the sand, but nothing happened.

"Over there!" exclaimed Fox. "I can hear it echo the notes."

"Where?" asked Chantel.

Fox flew down and landed on a small heap of sand. "Here, Chantel."

She ran towards him, kneeled down and sifted through the sand with both hands until she felt something hard. Her fingers closed around it, and she pulled it out.

"The Enchanted Medallion, the relic of the desert! How did you hear it?" she asked.

"My sensitive ears. I can hear the slightest sounds, even the sound of the beating wings of a night moth," Fox explained.

Chantel held the Medallion close to her ears. She could still hear its faint echo of Etam Luos's song. "Thank you, Fox," she said as she hung the beautiful wooden Medallion around her neck again.

"Well done, Princess," praised Eno.

Chantel blushed. She tried to get up, but her legs gave out from under her. She tumbled over and fell to the ground. She had held on to the power for too long. The fight and the excitement had distracted her, and the power had drained all her inner strength.

The Mighty Warrior helped her up. Eno took Chantel's water bottle and moistened her lips. Chantel's breathing gradually become stronger, and she opened her eyes. She was dizzy and her head hurt.

"That was close," she said in a small voice. "Thanks to your teachings, Eno, I found my way back."

"Remember, one day you will be powerful enough to use your power without the Magic Staff. But even then the power could still overwhelm you, so you must be careful," said Eno.

"I will. What will you do now?"

"I must find Etam and unite the lost tribes. Enim may be dead, but the true Evil One is not. I want the people of the South to be ready to help you if needed."

"Thank you, Eno."

"No, thank you, Princess. Without you I would be still hiding out on Storm Mountain with nothing but darkness inside me."

As Chantel and Eno hugged, Ilsole flew down to say good-bye to Eno, too. The Mighty Warrior changed back into Mouse and looked at Tac.

"I guess you will be going with her," he said.

"I must," said Tac.

"I hope I'll see you again, my friend," Mouse said.

"I'm sure you will. One day we will fight side by side again," Tac replied.

"I would be proud to fight with you again," said Mouse. "Farewell, Tac."

"Farewell, Mouse."

And with that, they all parted ways.

Mouse changed back into the Mighty Warrior and joined the others who had already started walking north. He picked up Chantel with his large paws and started to run. Ilsole and Fox took to the air and hastily followed above them.

The Mighty Warrior ran for the rest of the day, and just as the last sunrays touched the tops of the high mountains, they reached the familiar old oak tree.

"We made it!" yelled Ilsole. He and Fox were the first ones to land on one of the tree's big branches. They watched as the Mighty Warrior gently put Chantel down and changed back into Mouse. Chantel stood for a few seconds to collect her thoughts and balance. She felt much better and was able to climb up the tree by herself.

"I have some flat bread in my backpack," said Ilsole.

Fox flew down to Chantel and landed on her shoulder. Whenever he did that, Chantel was reminded of Laluna.

"Now, where is the food?" said Mouse. "I'm as hungry as a wolf. The desert is definitely too hot for me."

They enjoyed a quiet meal together and relaxed in the cold breeze that came down from the North.

"Let's get some rest," Chantel finally said. "We still have a long journey ahead of us before we reach our castle."

CHAPTER THIRTY-FIVE

Connected

Chantel woke up early. The sun just started to rise in the East. She climbed up higher into the tree. She looked south and thought about all that had happened during the last few days. Storm Mountain wasn't visible; it was too far away for her to see, but she thought about her time there with Eno. She remembered how she had lost her Soul Mate, how she had been rescued by her worst enemy, and how, best of all, she had brought the Inner Light back to the Wise One of the South.

"I will never let my Inner Light go out," she vowed. Before she turned to face north, she took a long last look at the desert as the first sunrays touched the glittering endless yellow sand. "What will happen next, I wonder?"

"Something terrible. I guarantee it!" said a voice in her head.

"How come you are filled with so much hatred, Spirit of the West?" thought Chantel.

"So you know who I am!" exclaimed the Evil One.

"Clever girl. You would be filled with hatred, too, if you had experienced what I have."

"What have you experienced?" asked Chantel calmly. "Why are you trying to kill me?"

"I am not trying to kill you, Chantel. I need you. You can control the light and the dark powers. The dark power connects us; that is how we can communicate. Nobody else can hear us. You and I are very much alike. I only have to convince you of that."

"That isn't true!"

"Yes it is; you just don't realize it yet, but I will show you. Remember that satisfying feeling of killing your enemies? Remember your desire to use the gift I gave you?" the Spirit continued. "You are more like me than you think. I am not trying to kill you, but you have to experience more pain so that you can feel what I feel. And once you have felt all the pain in the world, then you will understand me and be with me."

"I am not like you!" Chantel asserted again. "I am not filled with darkness! I am only trying to protect the people I love!"

"Ha! You think you are so noble! So good and right! Prepare for sorrow, Last Descendant!"

"What do you mean?"

"Your quest is one for dreamers. Do you think people will remember what once was? They have removed themselves too far away from nature. They destroy nature; they kill what keeps them alive. They are using you to save themselves, because they are afraid of me, and what I will do when I return. You are different because you are searching for the past.

You want to find out what happened to your parents. You want to remember, and I will help you remember everything when the time is right. We are very much alike, and I will soon show you how."

"No, we are not!" Chantel responded angrily.

"Chantel! Are you okay?" Mouse hopped down onto Chantel's branch. "Who are you talking to?"

"Was I talking out loud? I thought I was only talking in my mind."

"Were you visited by the Evil One?"

Chantel nodded. Her hands were shaking. "The Spirit of the West came to me again." Her upper lip was covered with small drops of sweat.

"Who?" Mouse whispered. He lost his balance and would have fallen off the branch if Chantel had not caught him by his paw.

"She said she will cause me a lot of pain so that I can understand her pain."

"The Evil One and the Spirit of the West are the same?" Mouse asked.

"Yes. In the desert, the Spirit of the South visited Etam and me. She told us all about the Spirit of the West," Chantel said. "But there is more you should know: Aquila Bellum saved my life in the desert. He rescued me from a sinkhole made by the Sand Divers. I don't know why, but I believe that he is fighting against his dark side."

Mouse listened quietly as Chantel explained everything.

"I'm glad you told me," he said after Chantel had finished. "No matter what happens or what we may learn, I'll always be with you."

"Thank you, Mouse," Chantel responded. She calmed down after having told Mouse about her fears, but what the Spirit of the West had said still troubled her.

The morning was cold, and the air was filled with the smell of dew and pine trees. Mouse climbed down the tree to look for food.

"I love the green valleys and the sight of the high mountains." Mouse smiled. "Come down! You will love the taste of these worms and crickets. They were hard to find. Soon winter will come, and then there'll be no more worms or crickets."

Chantel, Fox and Ilsole packed their few belongings and climbed down from the big tree. They had a quick breakfast of the last of the bread and were on their way before the sunrays touched the tip of the old oak tree.

"Tomorrow we will be at the castle again," Mouse said. "I wonder how Fin is doing. I hope he's feeling better and has fought off those dark thoughts."

"I hope so, too, Mouse," Chantel said.

Their travels went very well that day; they all enjoyed being in a more pleasant climate again.

Chantel thought about the banished spirit's ominous words. She thought about the time she'd spent with Eno Esiw and Etam Luos, but most of Chantel's thoughts were occupied by Aquila Bellum. She wondered what had happened to him. She felt that he was still alive, but she had no idea where he was.

CHAPTER THIRTY-SIX

Haunted by Memories

All that we have experienced will stay with us forever. Sometimes we can suppress our worst memories, but if the situation and the circumstances are right, they can resurface. It is good that the human being can forget; otherwise she will remember all the pain from being hurt and from bad times. But there is some pain that will never leave us. Those who have done wrong know what I mean.

From The Book of Erebus

Aquila Bellum wandered around in a daze. The explosion that had killed Enim Ymene had thrown Aquila a long way through the air. He had landed violently on his back and had been knocked unconscious. When he awoke, he was covered with dust and sand. It was dark, and he had no idea where he was.

Reorienting himself with the help of star constellations, he realized that he was close to the border of the land of the North—his land. He concentrated to try to find any evil ones in the area, but he had no luck. He couldn't even sense his wolverine.

"After that explosion, everyone is either dead or in hiding," he muttered to himself. "I will try again tomorrow."

His black cloak hung from his body in shreds. He ripped it off and threw it away. He found his sword beside him in the sand.

"Why didn't Enim use the power in the Enchanted Medallion to kill the Wise One of the South?" he thought angrily and started to walk north. "And why didn't I let Chantel die when the Sand Divers caught her? Enim was obviously experiencing the same doubts I feel. Will these doubts eventually kill me, just like Enim's doubts killed him?"

As Aquila began his journey home, he recalled Chantel's relieved smile after he had rescued her, when they were lying side by side. He had seen that same smile before—his sister's smile after he had pulled her to safety. His thoughts traveled back to his childhood. He saw his parents and his sister. They smiled at him like only proud parents and loving sisters do. He also heard their screams when they were trapped inside their burning house in the mountains. By that time, he had already turned to his dark side and was under the influence of the Evil One. He was twenty-five years old and his sister was twelve when she and his parents died. He had watched without any emotions as the fire he had started burned them to death.

Aquila heard their screams over and over again. He covered his ears, but the screaming did not stop. They were calling his name.

He started to run. He tried to run away from his past, but no matter how fast he ran, he knew that he could not escape it. What he had done would be with him forever.

CHAPTER THIRTY-SEVEN

Darkness in the Castle

Chantel, Mouse, Fox and Ilsole approached the forest that surrounded the castle. The leaves had already started to change colors. When Chantel had left for her journey to the South, the leaves still had a slight green tinge. Now they were yellow and red, and many had fallen from the trees and lay scattered on the ground. Chantel could sense winter coming, and she could sense something else: the Darkness.

"Over there," Chantel explained to Ilsole, pointing her hand at the small hill. "My castle is hidden behind a shroud of mist that makes it invisible."

"The Darkness is very strong here," Ilsole said. "I can feel it coming from the castle, Chantel."

"I can, too," Chantel replied. Her braid was hanging heavily and her neck tingled, as if crawling with ants. She had had that feeling once before, when Fin was crouched on the chair in the kitchen the day she had returned from the mountains.

"We must be sensing Eronimus Finsh, the Wise One of the North. Remember what I'd told you, Ilsole?" interjected Fox. "How jealous Fin had become of Chantel because she had the power to release the red lightning bolt?"

"We'd hoped that with time he'd remember his values and leave the Darkness," added Mouse. "I guess he hasn't yet."

"Are you sure leaving the Darkness is even possible?" asked Ilsole.

Thinking of Aquila, Chantel nodded hopefully. "I'm sure it is."

"What happens if the Darkness you feel now isn't coming from the castle but nearby? What if one of the evil ones is watching and waiting for you? We'd better be careful," said Mouse.

"Let's end our journey the way we began it," said Chantel. "Mouse, you hide in my pocket, and Fox, you sit on my shoulder. I will use the blue light to make us all invisible. That way no evil ones will see us. Ilsole, you'd better stay here until we come back to get you, because I don't know how Owl will react if he sees a Winged One."

"I could do that, Chantel, but I won't," Ilsole responded.

Chantel, Mouse and Fox looked at Ilsole with confusion, slightly irritated by his strong and determined voice.

"What do you mean?" Chantel asked.

"I have to find Laluna. I can't stay here and do nothing. There is so much I have to tell her. The future of the remaining Winged Ones depends on her. And there is someone very special waiting for her." Ilsole stood quietly even though his hands were twitching with excitement and the desire to leave.

"I know how you feel. I miss Laluna very much." Chantel saw Laluna's soft, kind face in her mind; she saw her lying on the ground, covered with blood and her colorful wings twisted. Tears welled up in her eyes. "You have to fly north, towards the waterfall tumbling down in the distance," Chantel explained. She didn't want to let Ilsole go, but she had to. She couldn't hold him back. "Once you are above the trees, you will see it. Mother Nature lives near that place, but I don't know if you will be able to contact her."

"I have to try. Thank you, Chantel."

"Be careful, my friend," said Fox. "Many enemies are awaking, and more are joining the Darkness every day now."

"Avoid the shadows. And at night, sleep in old oak trees that are plentiful in the North. The ones who have joined the Darkness do not dare to climb them, because the oaks are solid in their beliefs, and their alliance to Mother Nature can't be changed," Mouse added.

"Thank you, Fox. Thank you, Mouse, for the advice. I will see you soon again."

He gave Chantel a loving hug, opened his wings, and lifted up into the sky. Above the trees he turned north and quickly disappeared from sight. Mouse jumped into Chantel's cloak pocket, and Fox settled on her right shoulder. The crystal at the end of Chantel's Magic Staff lit up in blue, and in the blink of an eye, Chantel and her passengers vanished.

CHAPTER THIRTY-EIGHT

It Can't Be True

When the truth becomes clearer and the realization of betrayal awakes, the feeling of trust shifts to the dark side. Doubt and vulnerability take over. The one who will find this book will eventually be ready to encounter right and wrong without prejudging, because the one will have experienced all, including pain, suffering, helplessness and betrayal. So be ready; when you read this book you will suffer more.

From The Book of Erebus

Owl was waiting for Chantel at the huge doors. He knew that she was coming; he had felt her presence. It was a talent that all Wise Ones had. He opened the doors just as she lifted her hand to knock.

"Welcome back," he exclaimed. "I am so happy to see you again." Spreading his big gray wings, he hugged Chantel.

"It is good to be home again, Owl," said Chantel, burying her face in his soft feathers, ignoring the growing weight of her golden braid.

"Welcome, Mouse, Fox. You have protected our Princess well. Come into the kitchen and tell me all about your journey. I have prepared tea for you."

"How did you know that we were coming?" Chantel asked.

"I didn't," Owl lied. "Since you left, I have prepared tea every day in the hope that you would return that day."

In the kitchen, a plate of fresh, warm cookies sat cooling on the table, and a pot of water was hanging over the fire. "How could I ever have doubted Owl?" Chantel wondered. Chantel was happy to be home again. She loved this castle and was looking forward to seeing her tower again. Everything was as it always was. There is comfort in familiarity, and Chantel felt it.

"It smells delicious, Owl," Chantel said, "but do you mind if I have a quick bath and get changed before tea? I've had sand in my hair and ears for days now."

"Of course," replied Owl. "Take as long as you need."

Chantel hurried up her tower to the fifth floor. She did need a bath and a change of clothes, but there was something else she wanted to do right away.

She moved the table and rug that hid the imprints out of the way. She saw the Golden Sword lying in its rightful place, surrounded by an indigo-colored light. It looked so beautiful, and warmth radiated from it. She read the blade's inscription again: "For Us to Share."

Chantel took the Enchanted Medallion off her neck and placed it on top of the protective shield above its imprint in the floor, two tiles below of the Golden Sword. The Enchanted Medallion sunk through the transparent shield until it came to rest in its imprint. A yellow light started to shine and surround it. "Simplicity," she heard the wind that blew around her tower whisper.

Chantel relaxed. She was glad of the protective lights and shield, for although it was wonderful and comforting to see Owl and her old room, her braid was heavy—much heavier than it had been outside the castle, which meant there was darkness around her. But her senses told her that no amount of darkness could pierce through the shield and light.

"I must ask Owl where Fin is," she thought. "I hope he's okay."

She replaced the carpet and moved the table back into place and walked over to the windows that faced the land of the East.

"My next destination, the green forest of the land of the East," she said. "I have to find the Forest People. They have *The Book of Erebus*. Perhaps that book will finally tell me what happened to my parents and why I am called the Last Descendent."

After Chantel had freshened up and put on new clothes, she returned to the kitchen where she found Owl, Mouse and Fox sitting at the huge table. They were laughing about a story Mouse was telling. A warm fire was burning in the fireplace, and it made a comforting crackling sound. She sat down beside Owl on the bench.

"Where is Fin, Owl?" Chantel asked. "How is he doing?"

"Fin isn't doing well at all," Owl said, lowering his head.

"I had put him in one of the cells in the basement the day you left."

"I didn't know that there are cells in the castle," Chantel said, surprised.

"Yes," Owl said with a composed voice. "They were built a long time ago—a very long time ago. One of the bars had rotted, and Fin escaped. I tried to find him, but I couldn't."

"Aren't you worried that he might run to the evil ones and give away the location of the castle?" Mouse asked.

"No, not really," Owl said. "Since you left, he had problems orientating himself. He was constantly talking to himself, but nothing he said made sense. He was going mad. The last time I brought him a meal, he was so confused that he couldn't even remember his own name."

Chantel gulped. Perhaps Fin had lost his mind because he'd been imprisoned. If only Owl had told her where he was putting Fin; she would have never let him be put in a prison. Fin may have turned to the Darkness, but he wasn't fully or truly evil. With his mind blocked, he was quite harmless. Now he could be in danger.

Mouse, seeing Chantel's dismay, made a sign to her.

"I think . . . I think I need some fresh air after that news," said Chantel. She got up and walked out the door that led into the center courtyard.

"I'd better make sure she's okay," said Mouse, hopping off the table and following her outside.

Owl nodded, swallowing an entire cookie. He had seen the short eye contact between Mouse and Chantel and knew what was going on.

He could feel Chantel's suspicions about him.

"Strange," Mouse said when he reached Chantel. They were far enough away from the kitchen that there was no chance they could be overheard. "If Fin is not in the castle, whose presence did Ilsole feel? Whose presence do you feel?"

"I don't know, Mouse," Chantel answered, thinking of the dream she had had when she was with Etam. "I hope it's not . . . "

"We have to find more evidence before we come to any conclusions," Mouse said, trying to calm Chantel.

"Thank you, Mouse," Chantel said, blinking her eyes to hold off tears. "We should start on our next quest as soon as we can. And I must try to contact Mother Nature."

"What about the relics. Will they be safe here?"

"Yes. They are hidden well and protected by their own power. I am the only one who can retrieve them again."

When they returned to the kitchen Chantel's eyes were red.

"Come over here, my Princess," Owl said, opening his big gray wings to give her a hug. "I did not know that the bad news about Fin would affect you so much. I am sorry."

"Me, too," Chantel said.

As she hugged Owl, tears began to run down her cheeks. Owl tried to comfort her but did not realize that her tears were meant for him. Chantel's mind told her that Owl was an evil one, even though she could not understand why and did not know what had happened to Owl, but deep in her heart she knew that Owl would never harm her.

CHAPTER THIRTY-NINE

Patience

Aurora had met with the council, and now the council wished to meet with Fin. Eronimus Finsh knew that he was not in good standing with his people. He had neglected them far too long, and he could not expect that they would be excited to see him again. He still remembered well why he had turned his back on them: it was all the bickering and complaining that had started up after Aquila held the Golden Sword twenty moon crossings ago and released the red lightning bolt. The elders still blamed Fin for awakening the Evil One since he was the one who had presented the Sword to the Snow Walker that evening.

"I have to forget their ignorance," he told himself, "for Chantel's sake."

He felt ready to leave his room and walked around the beautiful castle of ice. As he encountered some of his Mountain People, he could hear their whispers.

"Is that supposed to be our Wise One?" they asked each other. "What does he want? He no longer belongs with us."

No one would talk to him directly or even acknowledge his presence. After a while he felt quite agitated and returned to his room.

"What am I doing up here?" he wondered. "I do not belong here anymore, and they do not want me around. They must think I am a bad omen." But then he remembered Chantel. She needed help. He couldn't give up. "A Wise One doesn't give up!" he thought.

But he felt lonely and longed for his cave beside the big waterfall. He would be lonely there too, but he would not be constantly reminded of it. He was used to the life of a hermit. He would have to relearn how to behave among his people if he were to stay any longer.

"The Mountain People are my people," he thought, "and I know that something will happen and that they are in danger. I have to gain their confidence again. They have to send their soldiers to help Chantel."

It took the wounded wolverine several days to reach Aquila's cave. His fur was covered with snow, and icicles crusted his fur. He was hungry, and the pain in his shoulder was intense. The bleeding had stopped, but the shaft of the arrow that had struck him was still deeply embedded in his flesh. He had tried to contact Aquila and the Evil One on his way back to the cave, but his wild, instinctive mind wasn't meant to focus on tasks besides hunting and killing.

Once inside the cave, he lay down, and Aquila Bellum's aroma awoke his memory of the Warlord of the North. He tried to concentrate on his image. He saw his master's face in his mind and growled in the old dialect, *"Master, where are you?"*

"Who is calling using the old tongue?" the Spirit of the West replied. Aquila couldn't hear his wolverine because he was lying unconscious below a pile of dust and sand.

"It is Rebus, the Warlord's hunter. I have found the den of the uprights."

"The Mountain People's hiding place. At last!" the Spirit of the West thought. *"Tell me, Rebus!"*

"The uprights are living below the wanderers of the sky."

"Very good. I am proud of you. You have done well."

"I am filled with pain. The wood of the uprights hurt me. Tell my master. He has to know. I can feel the long winter night coming."

The Spirit of the West didn't respond. She didn't know if Aquila was still committed to her and decided that she would not let Aquila know about the Mountain People's hiding place, at least not now. If he proved his loyalty to her, then she might tell him.

"I will organize the evil ones of the North myself and order them to attack the Mountain People. I will not wait any longer. They will all die," she thought. "And I will get part of my revenge sooner than I had thought."

She tried to contact Aquila's hunter again, but she didn't get any response. She wanted to tell him not to contact Aquila. She worried that if Aquila found out what she knew he might warn the Mountain People, but her worries were unfounded. Rebus's lifeless body lay in Aquila's cave. The only one he had been able to contact before he died was the Evil One herself.

CHAPTER FORTY

The Desert Song

After enjoying some more tea, Chantel excused herself and went to the top floor of her tower. She stood at the window facing west and watched the sun set beneath the mountains, first turning the sky orange and then red and finally purple. The green valley filled with a soft evening fog that made it look like a lake.

When the sun had set, she walked down one level to her bedroom, put her cloak on the floor, and lay down on top of it, using her backpack as a pillow. But she could not fall asleep; too many thoughts spun through her head.

She could have used advice from Laluna right now. She also thought about Owl and what she should do.

"What if I am wrong? He would feel so betrayed, and I would feel so ashamed. And what if I am right? He might attack me and try to kill me." Chantel shook her head. "No. He wouldn't. I know he wouldn't. He loves me, and if you love somebody you wouldn't hurt them. I sense his love for me, but he is also filled with darkness. I don't understand.

Tomorrow I will have to face Owl and find out the truth," she told herself. "I will talk to Mouse first so that he is ready, just in case I need him."

She tossed and turned for a long time. She finally got up and walked to the north-facing window.

The mountains were not visible even though the two moons were shining. The clearness of the sky reminded her of the night she'd spent with Etam, playing for the desert creatures.

She was still wearing the flute around her neck. Her fingers curled around Etam's treasured reed, and she raised it to her lips.

She started to play the desert song, which reminded her of Etam and the friends she had made in the desert. She knew now that she was not alone on her quest. All were involved to save nature and the four lands.

⁓✣⁓

The wind picked up the notes Chantel created and carried them south, deep into the desert.

Etam had found a place with shade and food. Two Desert Runners were with him. The Spirit of the South had told them where to find him, and they had carried him to their home, a small cave at the outskirts of the desert. His head still rang with the moans and groans of the Lost Ones, and his body still hurt from the red lightning bolt's explosion. He was trying to heal himself by meditating and resting, but he was weak and sad. He had not only lost his Soul Mate but also some of his talents. He was sure that he would eventually fully recover, but it would be weeks before he would be able to travel again.

The wind that came from the North made him smile.

"I hear your song, Chantel," he said calmly, listening, "but I can't help you or talk to you—not yet."

Someone else heard that beautiful song. Mother Nature listened carefully. She knew that Laluna had to recover or the prophecy would not be fulfilled. Mother Nature heard the pain that was hidden in the song, and she knew that it was Chantel playing the reed flute.

"I hear your lonely song, Chantel. The time of being patient and letting nature take its course is over. I can't wait any longer. Laluna has to heal faster."

CHAPTER FORTY-ONE

Sacrifice

The time will come when we all have to make sacrifices, but to what extent is one willing to do this? Think about that, since you must know. You will have made many sacrifices for people you do not even know or will never even meet. So why did you do it? Heroism, to gain respect, or pure selfishness to overcome your own fear? Make up your mind, because one day you will find out and you might not like what you will learn.

From The Book of Erebus

Laluna was up and wandering around in Mother Nature's cave when the rune stone on her friendship bracelet lit up.

"Chantel," she thought. "I miss you so much."

Mother Nature was watching Laluna as the girl walked carefully across the uneven ground. She smiled and was happy about the progress and recovery Laluna was making. Laluna had paid a high price for her loyalty. She had made many sacrifices for her friends and for her beliefs. Mother Nature saw the pain in Laluna's face with every step she took with her right wing hanging lifelessly from her back.

"I will make you whole again," Mother Nature thought. "Your sacrifices have not been made in vain, and you will no longer suffer. I have to do something now. We are running out of time."

"Come here, Laluna, please," Mother Nature said softly. "I have a very special treat for you."

Laluna looked at Mother Nature and smiled. Laluna slowly turned around and carefully walked over to her. She did not want to show it, but her face was tense and the pain was visible in her eyes. Each step she made was filled with agony and uncertainty about her future.

"What is it, Mother Nature?" she said in a whisper.

"I will prepare a special bath for you, a bath that has not been prepared for a Winged One for many, many moon crossings."

"Thank you, Mother Nature. That is very kind of you," Laluna said tiredly, almost like she was in a daze.

Mother Nature took Laluna's hand and carefully led her deeper into her cave. They reached the small lake with crystal-clear water in which Mother Nature had found her strength again.

"Please walk to the center of the lake, where you will find a boulder below the water surface. Sit on the boulder and wait," Mother Nature said. "It was not too long ago that I went through this ceremony," she thought.

Laluna followed the instructions and walked into the lake. She sat down on the boulder, and the water reached up to her chin. She felt as if she were floating. The water was comfortably warm, having the same temperature as her body. Her muscles started to relax, and her eyes became heavy.

She drifted off into a peaceful, faraway place. She saw wonderfully shaped clouds in a blue sky as she lay on a field that smelled like roses and lilies. The floating seeds of the poplar trees were in the air. All her pain was gone.

Mother Nature watched Laluna as she crossed over to the field of dreams. She lit a few purple candles, which she floated on top of the water. They drifted across the lake, their lights reflected by the dark crystals that hung from the ceiling of the cave. Mother Nature sat down on a rock at the shore of the lake. She started to concentrate. Her mind drifted far away, and she called upon all of nature's healing powers. The light in the dark crystals intensified and became brighter and brighter until everything in the cave—the lake, Laluna, the crystals and Mother Nature—became one.

Mother Nature transferred some of her natural powers to Laluna. She gave up some of her strength to save the Winged One.

Suddenly the crystals went dark, and only the lit candles that floated on the water provided a dim light.

Mother Nature opened her eyes slowly. In the last few minutes, she had aged many moon crossings. Silver streaks were visible in her hair and wrinkles crossed her face. Laluna was still suspended in a wonderful faraway place.

"Laluna," Mother Nature said softly. "Laluna, it is time to return. Come back and open your eyes."

A few quiet moments passed before Laluna slowly opened her eyes.

"That was so beautiful," Laluna said. "I felt no pain, no hunger, no thirst and no fear. What happened?"

She stood up slowly and walked towards Mother Nature.

"I feel no more pain. I can walk straight again. I feel like I did before that horrible attack." Laluna jumped up and down. The water splashed everywhere. She looked into Mother Nature's eyes and noticed the change in her.

"What have you done?" Laluna asked, realizing the sacrifice Mother Nature had made.

"The greater good sometimes requires small sacrifices," Mother Nature explained. "I have plenty of time to recover. Nature is very patient, whereas you are needed right now. Go and get ready."

"I hope Chantel will free us from the Darkness," Mother Nature thought. "Nature is suffering, and so am I. I had to lie to Laluna; she is too young to understand. Time is quickly running out, for me and nature. I can feel it."

"Thank you, Mother Nature," Laluna said. "Thank you for everything."

Laluna walked out of the lake and started to run. She grabbed her few belongings and made her way through the cave and its many stairs and plateaus. Finally she reached the top and climbed through the patch of moss that covered the entrance. The sun was high in the sky, and Laluna took a deep breath of the fresh mountain air. She opened her wings and slowly moved them back and forth and then faster and faster. Her feet lifted off the ground, and Laluna flew higher and higher until she reached the top of the tallest tree. She smiled and yelped for joy at the top of her lungs. Tears of happiness ran down her cheeks. Her colorful wings glittered in the sun.

"I made it!" she yelled.

She flew up, down, sideways and in circles. When she reached the ground again she slumped over, breathing hard.

"Chantel, my sister," she said, regaining her composure, "I will see you again very soon."

Her arm pointed south, and the rune stone on her friendship bracelet started to glow.

She ran to an old rock, jumped on it with one foot and pushed herself into the air. Her wings opened, and she flew higher and higher in an ever-growing circle. Finally she turned south and flew towards the castle hidden behind the mist and towards her sister.

⌐᠁⌐

On a rock near the opening through which Laluna had reentered the outside world, a creature sat very still. A dark tree shaded the area so that Laluna hadn't seen what lay hidden there. The creature watched her flight and got in position to follow her.

⌐᠁⌐

The next morning the cold mountain wind howled around Chantel's tower. Chantel was still thinking about Owl.

She didn't understand, but then there were so many things she no longer understood. Before her twelfth birthday everything was so easy and so clear. It was only she and Owl and nothing else. Back then she didn't know about the Darkness, she didn't know about Mother Nature or Mouse, and she didn't know about the Evil One, the Spirit of the West. Since then everything had changed. Now she had lied and felt pain and sorrow. She had used the Evil One's power and she had killed. She looked at the Magic Staff that lay on the table in the middle of the room, and a slight orange light began to flicker in its crystal. Chantel averted her eyes, but the shine became brighter until it filled her room. "You can use it to find out what Owl is thinking," a voice tempted. "But be careful; the Evil One is watching."

"No," vowed Chantel. "I won't. I will find out soon enough. I am stronger than my desires and will not be tempted again."

A tingling sensation raced through Chantel's body, and she stood up. A bright light shone from her wrist, and Chantel had to avert her eyes. She raced to the north-facing window and looked at the mountains.

"Laluna!" she yelled. "Laluna is coming!"

Epilogue:

As time progresses and the world around us changes, are we part of what is happening or are we the cause of it? Will we ever be able to fill the void that our destruction leaves behind, or will we one day regret the pain we caused? One thing is certain—time will never stand still. But it sometimes passes faster and sometimes slower. We are now entering one of those phases.

From The Book of Erebus

End of Book Two

The complete story of Chantel's Quest consists of